something SECRET

Gwyneth Rees is half Welsh and half English and grew up in Scotland. She went to Glasgow University and qualified as a doctor in 1990. She is a child and adolescent psychiatrist but has now stopped practising so that she can write full-time. She is the author of *The Mum Hunt* (winner of the Red House Children's Book Award for Younger Readers), *The Mum Detective*, *The Mum Mystery*, *My Mum's from Planet Pluto* and *The Making of May*, as well as the bestselling Fairies and Cosmo series and *Mermaid Magic* for younger readers. She lives in London with her partner, Robert, their daughter, Eliza, and their two cats, Hattie and Magnus.

Visit www.gwynethrees.com

Also by Gwyneth Rees

The Mum Hunt
The Mum Detective
The Mum Mystery

My Mum's from Planet Pluto
The Making of May

For younger readers

Mermaid Magic

Fairy Dust
Fairy Treasure
Fairy Dreams
Fairy Gold
Fairy Rescue
Fairy Secrets

Cosmo and the Magic Sneeze
Cosmo and the Great Witch Escape
Cosmo and the Secret Spell

Gwyneth Rees

something SECRET

MACMILLAN CHILDREN'S BOOKS

First published 1995 by Yearling Books

This edition published 2009 by Macmillan Children's Books
a division of Macmillan Publishers Limited
20 New Wharf Road, London N1 9RR
Basingstoke and Oxford
Associated companies throughout the world
www.panmacmillan.com

ISBN 978-0-330-46404-8

3 5 7 9 8 6 4 2

A CIP catalogue record for this book is available from
the British Library.

Typeset by Intype Libra Ltd.
Printed and bound in the UK by CPI Mackays, Chatham ME5 8TD

For Robert and Eliza, with love

Chapter One

I stared at the diary in Marla's hand.

'Did you read it?' I asked nervously.

Maria gave me her most severe look. 'Laura, I may be your mother's best friend, but I don't think that gives me the right to read her private diary, do you?' She stressed the word *private* as if she thought I might not have associated it with Mum's diary before.

I didn't answer. She'd caught me with the diary and she knew I'd read it. Now she was working really hard at trying to make me feel guilty.

'I realize your mother left for the airport a whole ten minutes ago, but, believe it or not, I haven't yet seized the opportunity to search through all her personal things. I suppose by your standards that's a bit slow, is it? I mean, there might be some more diaries, or some interesting letters we could read!'

I squirmed, despite not really feeling guilty. Marla can be very sarcastic when she's cross. This time though, she had no right to be cross. Not with me anyway.

'It's all Mum's fault,' I said defensively. 'If she'd told me the truth in the first place I wouldn't have had to go and read her stupid diary. I wish I hadn't read it anyway. It's . . . It's . . . HORRIBLE!'

I heard myself make an awful choking sound as I burst into tears.

'Laura, what are you talking about?'

I could hardly speak. I started taking short, sharp breaths. 'You know M-m-mum's sister, Kathleen?' I stammered between sobs.

'The sister who died in an accident when they were children?'

I nodded. 'Except that it wasn't really an accident!' I gasped. 'What really happened . . . What really happened was . . . Mum killed her!'

As soon as I'd said it there was a complete silence, as if Kathleen had dropped dead in front of us, right now, in this very room, instead of in some other room more than twenty years ago.

Marla sat quite still on the settee with an expression of complete disbelief on her face. 'Laura . . .' She was shaking her head in utter dismay. 'Laura, I can't believe . . .' Her voice dried up.

We just stared at each other dumbly.

It was very unusual for Marla to be speechless,

even if she couldn't believe something. It didn't last long.

'Laura, I can't believe that you can believe . . .' She pulled some tissues out of her pocket and threw them at me. 'I think you'd better stop crying and tell me the whole story.'

I gulped. I was feeling pretty speechless myself. I mean, finding out your mother is a murderer isn't even the sort of thing you always imagine happening to someone else but not to you. It's the sort of thing you can't ever imagine happening to *anyone*!

'Just start at the beginning,' Marla said firmly. 'Come on. You'll feel better. It's no good trying to bottle things up.'

I sniffed. I have to admit I've never been a great one for bottling things up . . .

Chapter Two

Mum never used to hide things from me. In fact, she always used to go on about how adults should try to be as open and honest as possible with children, rather than keeping them in the dark about things.

'It's far better for children to be told the truth, however bad, than to be left on their own imagining something even worse,' she used to say.

That's why, when I realized she was hiding something about Kathleen, I knew it had to be something far worse than she thought I could possibly imagine – and she knows I'm capable of imagining some pretty horrendous things.

I think it first crossed my mind that something was wrong round about the time when my best friend, Janice, started trying to persuade me to go to Guides with her. When Mum wasn't very keen on the idea, I didn't realize at first that it had anything to do with Kathleen. I just thought it was because Mum didn't think I'd like Guides. From the way Mum described it, I didn't think I'd like

Guides much either. Then Janice told me there was going to be a Guide barbecue in one of the parks, with a huge bonfire and an endless supply of sausages, and I had to admit that it did sound like a lot of fun. I told her I'd think about it.

Like I said, it wasn't as though I particularly wanted to be a Girl Guide before that. In fact, I used to tease Janice about it.

'What's fun about standing to attention in little lines while the Brown Owl or whatever she's called checks to see if you've got dirty fingernails? It sounds even worse than school,' I protested, twisting Janice's long red hair into a French plait so that she could wear it like that to Guides. I'd give anything to have hair like Janice's. My hair is blonde, which I quite like, but it's so frizzy it's impossible to make it stay in any sort of style at all.

'We don't have a Brown Owl – that's in the Brownies,' Janice said impatiently. 'Anyway, it's not like that. You don't know anything about it. My mum says it's really ignorant to sneer at something that you haven't even tried.'

'And my mum says that Brownies and Guides are guaranteed to stamp out individuality and self-expression and that they're religiously and culturally biased,' I retorted. My mother's quotes are always better than her mother's. They're just more difficult to remember.

No, I certainly wasn't bothered about missing out on Guides in the beginning. I'm not a lover of uniforms, and having to wear one to school is bad enough. I like to wear clothes that make me look cool, and there's nothing cool about a cream school blouse tucked into a navy pleated skirt, and an orange and blue striped tie that has to be worn at all times or else. I don't know who thought up the colour scheme for our school uniform, but it certainly wasn't anyone with any taste, and as far as I could see, the uniform they made you wear at Guides was ten times worse.

The other thing that put me off was that, according to my mother, Guides was chock-a-block with rules. 'All serving no other purpose but to make sure everybody is exactly the same as everybody else,' she said briskly, removing two rashers of bacon off the grill to feed to Rory, our cat, who was purring manipulatively at her ankles.

I crouched down to stroke him, gazing up at Mum, still trying to get used to how different she looked with her long messy hair transformed into a shiny black bob. It was Mum's friend Marla who had practically dragged Mum to the hairdresser's, and it was Marla who'd seemed most pleased immediately afterwards. 'What did I tell you? You look like a new woman! Doesn't she, Laura?'

I had nodded, awed by the change. Mum didn't look like Mum any more. I told her she looked like a model on one of those adverts for shampoo. 'It's not fair! Everybody's got nicer hair than me!'

Mum and Marla had both laughed. (Mum had been laughing a lot lately – almost as much as she used to when I was little and Dad still lived with us.)

She was laughing now as I solemnly asked Rory if he wanted eggs with his bacon. 'It is quite obvious that you are not Girl Guide material, Laura.' She ran her hand through her hair – she'd been doing that every five minutes since yesterday – and smiled at me approvingly.

'I suppose not,' I agreed, watching the cat tuck in to his once-a-week treat. 'Still –' I stood up – 'this barbecue sounds like really good fun. And they're going orienteering in the summer for a whole weekend and you get to sleep outside in tents.' I giggled. 'D'you think they'll have to rub sticks together to make a fire or d'you think they'll take matches?'

My mother said nothing. But the next day she was a bit late coming home from the hospital where she works, and it turned out she'd stopped off at our local community centre to enrol me in Scottish Highland Dancing classes. And it also turned out that these classes just happened to be on the same night as Janice's Guides.

It didn't bother me too much at the time. Mum is Scottish and although we live in England now she always goes overboard when it comes to celebrating Hogmanay and Burns Night, and if she gets really homesick she'll invite some friends round for dinner to eat haggis. (Haggis is really nice by the way, not at all like you'd imagine, considering what it's made out of.) So it didn't surprise me in the least when she seized on these classes as the best thing ever to arrive in Birmingham and insisted that I go, regardless of the fact that her own parents had forced her to go to Highland Dance lessons when she was my age and she'd always told me she absolutely hated it.

'Of course I didn't really hate it! I just thought I did at the time,' she said when I challenged her.

'Anyway I'd like to learn all the dances again. If you go you can come home and teach me.'

That was what made me agree to try it out – the idea of getting Mum to dance with me afterwards. And it turned out that I really enjoyed it. The class itself was good fun when you got to know the other people there, and I absolutely loved practising the Highland Fling with Mum when I came home. The two of us even gave a performance at Mum's next haggis party – Mum after much persuasion and several glasses of wine – during which all her friends nearly wet themselves laughing. All in all we were having the best time we'd had since Dad had left three years ago, and it certainly didn't bother me much that I was missing out on Guides.

Then one day everything changed.

'This is Hamish,' Mum said, stepping in through the front door and catching me still up two hours after our babysitter was meant to have sent me to bed. Cheryl, our babysitter, was hovering nervously behind me. She used to spend all evening trying to get me to go to bed and she was absolutely hopeless at it. She's the daughter of one of Mum's friends, so Mum finds it really difficult to get annoyed with her. I told Cheryl that Mum never gets annoyed because she's a psychiatrist and psychiatrists don't think sleep is very important. That was the biggest lie I've ever told, but well worth it. Now Cheryl doesn't hassle me much at all, unless she's got her boyfriend with her and wants to get rid of me for that reason.

'Hamish?' I queried loudly, half-expecting some little stray dog to follow her into the house, because Hamish sounded to me like the sort of name you'd give to a dog rather than a person.

'Hamish Fraser,' he said, stepping into the hall behind my mother. My heart sank. He had a Scottish accent. Mum's an absolute sucker for Scottish accents.

I took hold of the hand he was offering and shook it once. He wasn't as old as my dad and he wasn't going bald at the front like my dad either. He looked about the same age as Mum. (Mum is thirty-five this year and she says that from now on she is going to stay the same age for two years instead of one – that way it's going to take her another ten years to reach forty.)

'Laura, why aren't you in bed?' She was taking off her coat, her new red coat I noticed, the one she had spent three weeks debating whether or not to buy because it was so expensive and she'd never had anything that red before.

I turned and looked pointedly at Cheryl, which was a bit mean of me, but I figured she was getting paid for it.

'She was just going to bed, Doctor Rorison. I'm sorry. We lost track of the time.'

'Call me Sylvie,' my mother said as she always does when Cheryl gets flustered. 'Don't worry. It's all right. It's just that she's got school tomorrow. Now, how are you getting home? Have you got the car?' She turned to Hamish Fraser, who was taking his coat off too, despite the fact that nobody had invited him to. 'Cheryl passed her driving test last month, first time. I think that's amazing. It took me four goes and even then I'm positive they only let me pass because I was wearing the shortest skirt I could find.'

'I wonder if that technique would have helped me,' Hamish replied.

My mother laughed.

That annoyed me. It had been her joke, not his. He had only come in at the tail end of it. Besides, she seemed to have completely forgotten about me sitting on the bottom stair in my pyjamas losing more and more sleep by the minute.

'I haven't got the car tonight,' Cheryl interrupted

shyly. 'Mum and Dad are using it. I could just walk home. It's not that far.'

'I could give you a lift if you like.'

Mum and Cheryl both stared at Hamish.

Cheryl was about to speak when Mum said in a rush, 'It's all right. I'll do it. It won't take a minute. If you don't mind staying here with Laura, Hamish.'

That's when I made my move. I jumped up and thundered upstairs making more noise than ten stampeding elephants. How dare she suggest that! How dare she leave me on my own with him even if it was only for a minute! She was the one who was always going on at me not to go with strangers and here she was inviting one right into our house. He could be a murderer or a child-abuser or anything. I slammed my bedroom door. It would serve her right if I got straight on the phone to Child-Line.

I climbed into bed and lay there in the dark, listening to the sounds from downstairs. I heard the front door shut and then I heard some voices in the hall and then a bit later on I heard a car outside and the front door shutting again. Then everything went quiet. I must be in the house alone with him.

I rolled on to my tummy because I always sleep better that way, and tried not to listen out too hard for noises. Mum would be back soon. Hamish wasn't going to come upstairs. Tomorrow I'd tell Mum I didn't want her to leave me on my own with him again and she'd respect that. She always took me seriously about things like that, in fact she'd probably start apologizing and telling me how guilty she felt. Quite right too.

The stairs creaked. I froze. Then I heard footsteps on the landing and Mum's voice softly calling my name. So she hadn't gone out after all.

I sat up in bed just as the door opened and Mum came into my room.

'I've sent Cheryl home in a taxi,' she said. 'I wasn't thinking before. I'm sorry.'

'I thought you'd gone out and left me with *him*!'

'I've known him at work for a long time now, darling. He's one of the other doctors there. I would never leave you with a complete stranger.'

'He's a stranger to *me*!'

'I know. And we didn't mean you to get upset.' She came and gave me a hug and let me cling to her until I felt like letting go. Then she rearranged my duvet so that it covered me instead of being half off the bed. 'See you in the morning.'

I felt better, but not better enough to go straight off to sleep. I had this achy feeling inside me, like I really wanted something but I didn't know what it was. I stuck my thumb in my mouth – something I haven't done since I was about three – and shut my eyes.

Chapter Three

Hamish had been taking Mum out pretty regularly for several weeks and I felt like I was spending more time with Cheryl than I was with Mum.

I didn't mind too much at first. Cheryl showed me how to pluck my eyebrows (which is really painful) and how to do a French manicure (which takes absolutely ages, so if your babysitter ever offers to do it for you take my advice and turn her down). I really liked it when Cheryl brought her boyfriend with her. I only had to ask him one maths question and he'd end up doing all my maths homework for me, and he let me play leapfrog with him (which I was practising for gymnastics at school).

'You're going to break something!' Cheryl yelled as she deftly stopped Mum's favourite table lamp from toppling off the edge of the table I'd just knocked with my foot. 'Get upstairs and go to bed! Now!'

'OK, keep your hair on!' I giggled. 'You've still got at least an hour of snogging time before Mum gets back.'

Up in my room I switched on my CD of Scottish Dance music. I knew that even if Cheryl heard me practising – and I thump around a fair bit when I'm doing my Scottish Sword Dance – she wouldn't come and investigate. I used to think she must be hard of hearing, but I've come to the conclusion that she just pretends not to hear so that she doesn't have to bother doing anything about it. I can't say I blame her. If I was her I'd consider it a big enough achievement just to get me up the stairs and out of sight before Mum gets back. Anyway, tonight I needed to practise my dancing because I hadn't done any all week and my class was tomorrow. I found I wasn't practising as much now that Mum was always too busy to practise with me. It wasn't so much fun on my own.

I watched myself in my wardrobe mirror as I did the steps around the two wooden swords criss-crossed on the floor. Mum had made the swords herself out of some old bits of wood. She kept saying she was going to sandpaper the rough edges, but so far she hadn't had time – no prizes for guessing why.

I looked pretty silly jumping up and down in my green and red stripy pyjamas with my face all pink and my hair all messed up because I hadn't

tied it back like you have to at class. I tried to imagine what I'd look like in a kilt and one of those
white blouses with a frill down the front like you see
people wearing at Highland Dancing competitions.
I pulled a face at myself in the mirror and giggled.

In the mirror I spotted movement that wasn't
me. I instantly stopped dancing and turned round.
My bedroom door had been flung open.

'Laura!' It was Mum. She walked into my room
and turned off my CD player. 'What do you think
you're doing? It's way past your bedtime.' She was
wearing her red coat and a cream silk scarf that
Hamish had bought for her. She smelt strongly of
perfume. I decided I didn't like the way she looked
or the way she smelt.

'I'm practising. Not that you'd care.' I mumbled
the last bit but she heard me.

She shut the door and took off her coat, laying it
carefully over the edge of my bed. 'Let's get one
thing straight. I'm not putting up with the spoilt-
kid routine. OK?'

I stuck out my lower lip and refused to look at
her.

'OK, so tell me what's wrong.' She went a little
pink. She knew that I knew that she knew full well
what was wrong. 'Is it Hamish?'

'It's not Hamish, it's *you*. You're not the same. You don't even look the same. I hate that coat. I wish you'd never bought it. You look horrible in it. And that perfume *stinks*!' I bent down and lifted the wooden swords she had made for me. 'And it's no fun practising this on my own. You were the one who wanted me to do it in the first place. Ouch!' I winced as a sharp pain shot through my finger.

'What have you done?' She stepped towards me anxiously.

'It's a splinter. It's these stupid swords.' Seething, I started to suck at my finger with a ferocity Dracula would've been proud of.

'Let me see.' She dragged my finger out of my mouth, ordering me to stand still. 'You should be asleep in bed. If Cheryl can't make sure you're in bed at the right time then I'm just going to have to look for another babysitter.'

'No!' I screeched, tearing my hand away from her. 'I like Cheryl!'

'Of course you like her! She lets you stay up all night! Maybe if she was the one having to prise you out of bed in the morning—'

'Well, she'd probably do that too if you paid her,' I yelled.

I knew from the look on her face that I'd gone

too far. I jumped into bed and pulled my quilt up to my chin. 'I'm sorry,' I shrieked, but only because I was scared by how angry she looked, not because I meant it.

The only other time I could remember her looking like this was when we'd had a row about how I always spent a ridiculously long time on the phone to Dad (in Australia) and I'd ended up yelling at her that I'd go and *live* with Dad if she wanted and then she wouldn't have to worry about the phone bill. That time she'd looked angry enough to throttle somebody, though weirdly enough, her fury had passed almost immediately and *she* was the one who had ended up shrieking out an apology.

'I'm sorry,' she had burst out. 'Of course you must ring him! You must ring him whenever you want to! Here! Ring him again now if you like!'

I hadn't wanted to ring him back, because I'd been on the phone for so long already that I hadn't got anything left to say to him, but Mum was already punching in his number. 'It's OK, Mum. Really. I don't want to.'

'No. No. He's your father. You miss him. Of course you must speak to him. Where are you going? Come back.'

I slipped out the front door just as she got

19

through to Dad. I ran across the road to Janice's. Maybe while Mum and Dad were talking on the phone they'd discover they still loved each other. Maybe Dad would leave the new job he'd moved to Australia for in the first place and the new wife he'd met once he was out there and the new baby daughter they'd recently had together, and he'd come back to live with us instead. (What really happened, I discovered afterwards, was that Mum demanded to know why Dad didn't phone *me* more often and they'd ended up having a row fit to burn out all the telephone wires between here and Melbourne.)

I almost wished Mum had screamed at me tonight instead of just quietly leaving the room without saying another word. At least if she'd yelled she'd probably have ended up hugging me afterwards, which would've been a lot better than leaving things like this. She hadn't even kissed me goodnight.

I lay in bed in the dark, struggling with the way I felt about Mum. I was so angry with her but at the same time I loved her so badly. I never wanted to grow up and leave her. I never wanted the two of us to have to separate.

Hamish's deep laugh sounded from downstairs and I felt angrier still. He had no right to be sitting downstairs with my mother, laughing, while I lay up here all alone with my morbid thoughts and my throbbing finger. Everybody seemed to have forgotten about my finger. I poked at the splinter and made it hurt more. It might get infected overnight. I might get gangrene and die. What would they do then? Would Hamish laugh even louder? I imagined him at my funeral, pretending to be sad when really he was overjoyed because it meant he could have Mum all to himself. I imagined my mother standing at my graveside, dressed in black, her arms filled with flowers, leaning on Hamish for support. I imagined my father flying in from Australia, seeing my mother looking completely tragic and beautiful and realizing he still loved her. I saw him punching Hamish so that he fell into the hole they'd dug for my coffin, and then while he was lying on top of my coffin Hamish would hear a tapping sound and everyone would realize that I wasn't really dead after all, only unconscious, and they'd open up the lid and Mum and Dad would pull me out and the three of us would live happily ever after.

I suddenly realized that the tapping sound was real and that it was coming from the other side of my door. Sleepily I sat up in bed. 'Who is it?'

'Hamish. Can I come in?'

I froze. I'd only ever spoken to Hamish before when Mum was there, giving polite answers to his carefully-designed-not-to-give-offence questions. I'd never spent any time with him on my own and I'd certainly never allowed him inside my room.

I switched on my bedside light. 'Why?'

'I hear you've got a splinter in your finger. Difficult to get to sleep with a splinter in your finger. Want me to have a go at removing it?'

'Why?' What I meant was, why you and not Mum?

He was opening my bedroom door tentatively. 'I work in a casualty department. I'm always removing things from people's fingers or feet or eyes. I'm pretty good at it. You haven't got anything in your eye as well, have you? I could get that out at the same time.'

I couldn't help smiling, which he took as an OK to come right into my room. I had to struggle to change the smile to a frown. 'It's not a joke, you know. People can die from infected fingers. My friend Janice told me and she learned that at Guides.'

'She's absolutely right. An infected finger can be a very serious thing indeed. That's why I thought I'd better take a look. Do you mind?'

I glanced down at my finger. It didn't exactly look like it was about to turn into pus and fall off, but the splinter was still there and it was a bit pink. 'Wait a minute.' I got out of bed and put on my dressing gown.

We went into the bathroom and he ran my fingertip under the tap, then he sat down on the edge of the bath and peered at it.

'I know it's not that big,' I said defensively.

'It's not necessarily the size of these things that matters,' he replied solemnly, poking at it with one of my mother's sewing needles.

'Did you sterilize that?' I demanded.

His mouth twitched slightly. 'Believe me, Laura, I would never dare to approach you with anything less than a very sterilized needle.'

'Ouch!'

'Got it!' He let go of my hand and laid the needle down on the edge of the bath. We looked at each other. I suddenly felt really embarrassed.

'You'd better not leave that there. It might get knocked off and somebody might get it stuck in their foot.'

I regretted saying that as soon as I'd said it. It sounded really childish and ungrateful, which was exactly how I felt, but I didn't want Hamish to know that.

Hamish was looking at me as though he thought it would serve me right if he stuck that splinter right back in my finger. 'Oh, that's no problem. Taking a needle out of somebody's foot is even easier than removing a splinter. A needle is much bigger, you see. Much easier to grab hold of with tweezers.'

'How are you two getting on?' Mum arrived in the bathroom doorway, a glass of wine in each hand.

'Fine,' Hamish said, smiling at her as he took one of the glasses.

'My finger is getting on fine,' I added, to clarify things. 'I think I'll go to bed now. I've got to get up for school in the morning.' I walked with dignity towards my bedroom. Before I closed my door I turned round and said carefully, 'Thank you.'

'Any time.' He grinned.

Lying in bed, I thought with great satisfaction about how reasonable I was being. I imagined my mother saying to Hamish, 'She's behaving so reasonably about this, isn't she? I was so worried at first.' Worried at first but not any more – was that the way I wanted it or not? I loved Mum and I wanted her to be happy, not worried, but at the same time, if being happy meant being with Hamish instead of with me . . .

Janice was good at getting splinters out. I should have waited until tomorrow and asked her. She wasn't at all squeamish about digging her fingernails into your skin and squeezing. I wondered if it was something you learned how to do at Guides along with learning how to put someone's arm in a sling and how to bandage up a sprained ankle. Janice was always practising that sort of stuff.

That night I had a really weird dream. I was dancing the Highland Fling in front of a huge audience and I couldn't understand why everyone was pointing and laughing at me until I realized I was the only one on stage wearing a kilt. Everyone else was wearing a Girl Guide uniform. Then I realized I wasn't meant to be doing the Highland Fling at all. I was meant to be standing to attention while my patrol leader inspected my fingernails. Desperately I scanned the hall for my mother and found her sitting next to Hamish (who was also wearing a kilt) in the front row. Her hand was resting on one of his horrible hairy knees. 'Mum, I'm in the wrong place!' I cried out desperately. But she was far too busy flirting with Hamish to hear me.

Chapter Four

It started to bug me that Mum was hardly ever in.

Cheryl kept telling me not to be jealous, which bugged me even more. It was OK for Cheryl. She was probably going to be able to retire soon on all the money she was making from babysitting me.

I decided it was time to let Mum know how I felt.

Mum always says that she never wants me to keep her in the dark about the way I'm feeling. Now, I'm not stupid. I know what she means is that I'm supposed to *tell* her how I'm feeling. The thing was, I didn't want to tell her. If I told her I was jealous of Hamish she wouldn't get rid of him. She'd probably suggest that the three of us sit down together and *all* talk about how we felt or something yucky like that. I didn't want to know how they felt. I just wanted them to know how *I* felt.

I tried phoning Dad and asking him, very loudly when Mum was in earshot, how easy it would be for me to go and live with him in Australia if I wanted to. Mum went into the kitchen and fixed herself a

very large gin and tonic, but she didn't say anything.

Then I told Mum that I was thinking of dropping out of the debating club at school. (Mum
really likes the fact that I'm in the debating club,
because she says if she'd got used to speaking in
public when she was my age she's sure she
wouldn't have been so shy as a teenager. Difficult
to imagine Mum ever being shy, but still . . .) Mum
looked solemn when I told her, and said that that
would be a shame, but she didn't go on about it.

I was feeling pretty fed up with her infuriatingly
calm reactions to everything I threw at her, when
something happened without any help from me at
all that made her go absolutely crazy.

I bounced into the kitchen one morning still in
my pyjamas even though I was meant to be getting
dressed ready for school. 'Guess what?'

She didn't turn round. I don't think she even
heard me. She was standing stirring something on
the stove, still in her dressing gown, her brand-new
dressing gown that looked like it didn't care if you
froze to death so long as you froze to death looking
sexy. Rory ('Rory Rorison!' Hamish had picked
up immediately, much to Mum's delight) was rubbing his body against Mum's ankles and mewing

pitifully. I saw by his empty bowl that she hadn't fed him yet. Normally she feeds him before doing anything else.

'What are you doing?' And more to the point, where was my breakfast? Where was the mug of tea that had always cooled to just the right temperature by the time I got downstairs to drink it? Where was the peanut butter on toast I always got hurled at me with an exasperated warning that I had two minutes to eat it if I didn't want to be late for school?

She glanced over her shoulder and smiled at me vaguely. 'Oh . . . Laura. It's you.' She looked like she was in a very happy trance.

'What's that?' I pulled a face as I peered into the pan.

'Porridge. Do you want some?'

'Porridge?' I decided Mum must have been wrong when she told me that madness wasn't catching. She had obviously caught it from one of her patients. There was no other explanation.

'It's for Hamish. This is what his mother used to make for him every morning on school days.'

I got a feeling inside me that I didn't like very much. '*My* mother used to make me peanut butter on toast on school days!'

Mum hates sarcasm and she won't usually let me get away with it. This morning she merely smiled and started humming.

I felt like screaming. I hadn't even realized Hamish had stayed the night. He'd stayed until five o'clock in the morning before, I knew that, because one night I woke up thirsty and when I went down to the kitchen to get a drink, Hamish was there, making cheese on toast. Staying the whole night was something else though. You stayed the whole night in a house when you lived there. Hamish wasn't going to start living with us, was he? Mum would discuss it with me first, wouldn't she? Since Dad left she'd discussed everything with me, from what colour I thought her new bedroom curtains should be to whether I thought our postman fancied her when he started ringing the bell to give her letters that could quite easily have fitted through our letter box.

'Go and get dressed, Laura, there's a good girl.'

I glowered at her. How dare she treat me like a five-year-old? It wasn't fair – just because she had Hamish now.

I left for school without bothering to tell her my news. I knew she wouldn't be listening properly anyway. She was too busy having a candlelit breakfast with Hamish in the kitchen.

By morning break I was starving and I was more than grateful for a half share in Janice's packet of crisps. I usually have an apple to eat at playtime – Mum is always going on about the sugar in sweets rotting your teeth and the fat in crisps blocking up your arteries – but this morning I'd forgotten to take one from the fruit bowl. I'd also forgotten to ask Mum for my dinner money. Janice offered to lend me some of hers, but I decided that as from lunchtime I would go on a hunger strike. I'd seen a film once where two children went on a hunger strike to stop the mother of one of them marrying the father of the other. The trouble was, I hadn't seen the end of the film to see whether or not it worked.

'It won't work,' Janice kept saying all morning. 'And anyway, if you starve yourself to death and they do split up then you won't be around to enjoy it, will you?'

That was true. 'Maybe I should just *pretend* to go on a hunger strike, not eat at home but make sure I eat when Mum's not around.' I thought longingly of the school canteen's apple crumble.

'Nah! Your mum's a psychiatrist. She'll be able to tell you're faking it.'

'Psychiatrists only know what their patients tell them – they can't read minds,' I said, which is what Mum always says whenever someone she knows starts treating her like she owns a crystal ball.

Janice still looked sceptical. 'She'll be able to tell anyway, because you won't be getting any thinner. You've either got to do it for real or not at all and if you do it for real you won't be able to have any of Mum's chocolate cake this afternoon.'

That clinched it. I wasn't going to miss out on apple crumble *and* chocolate cake both on the same day just because of Hamish. I'd have to think of another way to make my point. Maybe I should just tell Mum how I felt. Maybe I should tell her that for one thing I didn't approve of Hamish staying the night and for another I was absolutely furious that she'd made his porridge a priority over my peanut butter on toast.

After school I went home with Janice as usual, to wait until Mum got back from work. In the beginning Mum had tried to offer Mrs Bishop money for looking after me and they had nearly ended up fighting over it. It was really embarrassing, especially when Mum exclaimed, 'I couldn't *possibly*

31

expect you to do it for nothing!' I mean, is looking after me that big an ordeal, or what?

Nowadays though, Mum just accepts Mrs Bishop's help (even though I can tell it still bothers her). And I'm really glad she does because (like I keep telling Mum) I really like Mrs Bishop and I'd hate it if I couldn't keep going to her house every day after school.

Just as Janice had promised, her mum had made a chocolate cake while we were at school. I had two pieces (and didn't get sick or fat, which are Mum's two excuses for never letting me have more than one piece of cake at home). Mrs Bishop offered to give me the recipe so that Mum could make it for me, but I said that I doubted she would have time. 'Not unless chocolate cake is another thing Hamish's mother used to make for him when he was a wee boy,' I added sombrely.

Mrs Bishop looked like she was struggling not to smile. 'I'll give it to you anyway, shall I? Just in case.'

I like Janice's mum. She is calm and easy-going and she always has plenty of time to do things with you, like organizing a game or getting out her sewing machine to help with the aprons Janice and I both really hate making in design and technology at school. She's a good cook too. Whenever I think of Mrs Bishop I think of her standing over her stove, tasting things. She always spends lots of time tasting things. Janice and I reckon she must eat the equivalent of a whole dinner in spoonfuls every night before she even serves it up – and another whole dinner afterwards because she can't bear to throw away the leftovers.

'That's probably why Dad's so strict about us finishing everything on our plates,' Janice joked. 'Cos he's scared of Mum getting any fatter.'

Personally I think I'd prefer it if my own mother was a bit more relaxed about what she ate. She's always on a diet, which she's always breaking and blaming me for: 'I thought I told you to hide these chocolate biscuits! It only took me two minutes to find them at the back of that cupboard. If you can't hide them properly then we're just not going to buy any and that's that!'

I looked at my watch. Mum was usually here by now.

Mrs Bishop was telling Janice to go and change out of her school uniform. 'You know how cross Daddy gets if you're not changed by the time he gets home.'

I knew how cross he got. I'd seen him blow up at

33

Janice once. I'd have to have spray-painted all the walls in our house to make Mum yell at me like that. I've always been quite scared of Janice's dad. He is tall and skinny with a short greyish beard and eyes that never quite settle on yours when he's talking to you. Whenever I see him he's generally on his way to or from work wearing the same very smart grey suit and highly polished (by his wife) shoes. I once asked Janice what he worked as and she told me he had his own business. I'd argued that he couldn't have, because if he did he'd be able to wear what he liked to work instead of that horrible grey suit, which looked to me about ten times more uncomfortable than our school uniform.

'Well, at least he doesn't go to work looking like he's going to a fashion show, which is more than can be said for some people's parents!' Janice had retaliated.

I didn't rise to that. Knowing Mum, she'd take it as a compliment anyway. That morning she'd gone off to the hospital in the purple skirt she'd originally decided was too short to wear to work, but had changed her mind about after spotting Hamish in the casualty department. ('If I waste any more time one of those nurses will snap him up!')

34

The doorbell rang.

'That'll be Mum!' I followed Mrs Bishop out into the hall.

'Sorry I'm late,' Mum gasped. 'I had to go and see a patient in Casualty. I thought I was going to be stuck there all night.'

I scowled. You don't need half a brain to work out why every trip to the casualty department takes Mum twice as long as it used to.

Mum reached for my hand. 'Has she been good?'

'She's always good. She's been helping eat my chocolate cake, haven't you, Laura? I offered to give her the recipe but she says you don't have time to bake cakes these days.'

Mum laughed. 'Poor Laura's had a lot to put up with recently, haven't you, pet?' She squeezed my hand. 'I promise I won't make porridge for break-fast ever again. How's that?'

Encouraged, I embarked on what I'd been trying to tell her that morning. 'Mum, I've got a message from my dance teacher. I told Cheryl when she picked me up from class last night. Did she tell you about it when you got in?'

She shook her head. 'What was she supposed to tell me?'

'They can't get the hall on a Tuesday any more,

so they're going to change the night to Wednesday. That means I'll have Tuesday nights free now and that means I can go to Guides with Janice.'

Mum let go of my hand abruptly.

'I know I didn't want to go that much before, but I've been thinking about it – and about that barbeque they're having—'

'The biggest sausage sizzle in the whole of Britain,' Janice chipped in. 'All the Guide companies in Birmingham are going to be there.'

'Yes, and I really want to go, but you've got to actually belong to a Guide company, so if I join Janice's now—'

'I think not,' Mum said coldly.

'But that's not fair!'

'I'm not about to discuss it, Laura. I do not approve of Guides and that is final.'

'But it isn't fair—' Janice began.

'Janice,' her mother warned, but I could tell Mrs Bishop didn't think it was particularly fair either.

I stared at Mum. It was as if a mask had crept over her face, shutting everybody out, including me. I suddenly felt sick. Mum was looking just how she had looked after Dad left and I had spent days stomping round the house, crying, 'It's not fair!'

'You're right, Laura,' she had said stonily. 'It

isn't fair. It especially isn't fair on you. I'm afraid that's something you're just going to have to get used to about life – that it isn't always fair.'

I pushed past Mum, out through the door and down the front path. I wasn't even looking where I was going. If I'd looked I might have seen Mr Bishop's car instead of running out into the road in front of it.

Chapter Five

I stood absolutely still, inches away from the car bonnet.

What happened next was so crazy I could hardly take it in. This shouting, screeching, unrecognizably mad woman threw herself at me, grabbing hold of my arms and shaking me until I thought part of me was going to snap off. I got such a fright I started to cry.

'For God's sake!' Mr Bishop probably saved my life at that moment by climbing out of his car and shouting at both of us.

Mum stopped shaking me, but I continued to tremble anyway. My legs felt like the legs of a ninety-nine-year-old woman who's just run the London Marathon. If Mum hadn't been gripping my arms so tightly I think I'd have collapsed in a heap on the ground. Tears were streaming down my cheeks. My nose was all blocked up. I could hardly breathe. Mum's grip on my upper arms was so tight it felt like it was cutting off the circulation.

'Are you trying to get yourself killed, young

lady?' Mr Bishop's face was bright red. 'If I'd been going any faster—'

'Yes,' Mum interrupted, so hoarsely there was almost no sound there at all. 'Thank you.' The next minute she was propelling me at top speed across the road towards our house.

I found my voice. 'Mum, I'm sorry. I didn't mean to. I'm really sorry.' I tried to stop her dragging me forwards, but she was too strong for me.

She fished her key out of her bag with one hand – the other still gripping me tight – and fumbled to fit it in the lock. Giving up, she hurled the keys at me. 'You do it!' Her face was pure white.

Inside, she let go of my arm. My immediate instinct was to run away from her, but I resisted, not wanting to seal my fate before I even knew what it was. My arm ached with pins and needles. I stood clutching it while she took off her coat, drew the curtains and switched on the lamp in the front room, fumbling through each of these tasks like someone with twice the usual number of fingers on each hand.

When she finally turned to look at me her eyes were huge and very dark.

I couldn't stand it any longer. 'I've got loads of

homework,' I gasped, turning and fleeing up to my room.

I sat on my bed, hugging myself, praying that she wouldn't come upstairs after me.

What had happened out there? In my whole life Mum had never acted like that, not when I fell out of the tree in our back garden and broke my arm, not when I got stuck on the roof after climbing the ladder she'd been using to clean the upstairs windows, not even when I set my shoes on fire by trying to dry them under the grill. I'm not saying she didn't freak out on all those occasions – far from it – but it had definitely been my mother, Sylvie Rorison, freaking out. This time had been different. This time I had been accosted by a complete stranger.

I suddenly badly wanted to phone Dad.

It wasn't that I wanted him to help. Dad's far too far away to be any real help whatsoever. I know that. It would be torturing myself to start wishing he was here. I only ever let myself do that when I know I'm just about to see him again (and he's only been able to come back to see me once since he left, because the flights from Australia are so expensive). I just wanted to hear his voice, that was all. I wanted to check that he was still there,

40

still the same. I wanted him to tell me one of his rude jokes so I could repeat it to Mum and watch her screw up her face in disgust: 'Laura, I'm so glad to be reminded of just how awful your father's jokes are.'

As quietly as I could, I slipped through to Mum's bedroom to use the extension. I didn't have to look up Dad's number. I was proud of the fact that I knew it – including the code for Australia – off by heart. I picked up the phone.

'Maybe I should prescribe myself a tranquillizer!' Mum gave a hollow little laugh at the other end.

'Sylvie, do you want me to come over?'

The other voice was Marla's. I haven't really told you much about Marla yet, except that she's the only person I can think of whose advice Mum actually listens to. I can't imagine anyone else but Marla managing to persuade Mum to have her hair cut short. Marla lives in Birmingham too and she and Mum see each other almost every week. Marla got divorced the year before Mum and was the chief person Mum used to phone when all the legal stuff started with Dad. She's got one son, called Oliver, who's just gone away to college and she spends all her time worrying about whether he'll remember he's allergic to fish – I think I would if I came out in a great blotchy rash and nearly died of an asthma attack every time I ate the stuff – without her there to remind him.

'Marla, I completely lost control.' Mum was sounding really shaky. 'It was a complete flashback, like it was happening all over again.'

'Listen, pour yourself a gin. I'm coming over.'

'God knows what my poor little Laura must be thinking—'

I suddenly felt too guilty to keep on listening.

The instant I'd replaced the handset I regretted it. I wanted to find out more. Mum had mentioned a flashback – a flashback to what?

I picked up the phone again.

It was the dialling tone.

Frustrated, I went downstairs and stood in the hall for a while, listening. I couldn't hear anything at all. That was unusual. Mum usually switches on some music or the news or the microwave or all three as soon as she gets in from work. I'm always having to yell at her to turn down Rachmaninov – which I can't even pronounce – or Beethoven or the Beatles because I can't hear myself think to do my homework.

Tentatively I pushed open the door of the living room. 'Mum?' I whispered.

She was sitting curled up on the sofa, her shoes kicked off in the middle of the floor. She was staring down at something in her lap – a large flat book.

'Mum.'

She heard me that time and looked up. Her eye make-up was all smudged. Hastily, she ran her fingers under her eyes and put down the book. 'Laura.'

I badly wanted to run to her.

She stared at me for a couple of seconds. Then she held out her arms.

'I'm sorry,' I repeated over and over again, as if stopping saying it would stop her hugging me.

When finally she extricated herself, she held me before her at arm's length and said, very sternly, 'Don't ever do that again.'

I couldn't say anything. Relief was making my eyes fill up; relief that Mum was back again, my mum, the person I knew.

'When's Marla coming?' I mumbled.

'What?'

I could have kicked myself. 'I mean, is Marla coming? I mean, sometime? To see us soon?'

43

'Pretty soon,' Mum answered, staring at me hard. 'In about ten minutes, I should think.'

I blushed and looked down at my feet. I was treading on Mum's book. I saw then that the book wasn't really a book, not the kind you read, anyway. It was a photograph album.

I swooped down on it immediately. It was the album Mum hardly ever got out, the one with all the pictures of her when she was a little girl. I grinned as I found my favourite photograph. 'You look so funny with your hair in pigtails. Tell me again what happened when you let your hair out on the way to school and Kathleen told on you . . .' I stopped, sensing from her face that I'd said something wrong.

She tried to take the book. 'Not now, Laura.'

I held on to it, flicking the pages over to find the other photo I really liked, the one of Mum and her sister, Kathleen, standing side by side in their school uniforms, looking incredibly solemn and formal. Whenever I look at that picture I always feel especially drawn to Kathleen, maybe because I know it was the last photo taken of her before she died.

'Laura, please . . .'

I snapped the book shut and handed it to her.

Mum always found it difficult to talk about Kathleen without getting upset, which was a pity,
because I'd really have liked to have known more
about what happened to her. I knew she was two
years younger than Mum and that she was killed in
an accident when she was ten. I knew that nobody,
not Mum, not Granny and not Grandpa before he
died two years ago, could ever say her name with a
steady voice.

I looked up at Mum now, starting to think.
Killed in an accident? A road-traffic accident?
Knocked down by a car, maybe? I longed to ask
questions, but if you'd seen the look on Mum's face
right then you'd realize why I just couldn't. I was
frightened I'd make her cry.

I was really glad when the doorbell rang.

'That'll be Marla.' Mum looked relieved too.
'Now go and get changed out of that school uniform. Do you realize you've got chocolate icing all
down the front of that blouse? Here. Put this away
for me.' She gave me the photo album.

As I got changed I hoped Marla was doing a
good job of cheering Mum up. Marla usually had a
whole stack of stories about Oliver that make my
escapades seem trivial in comparison. With any
luck she'd be relating a particularly awful one

right now. Maybe Oliver had eaten some fish as part of a student demonstration and been arrested by the police and had a hypersensitivity reaction in the police cell. He might even have been rushed to hospital in an ambulance. What if a special fish antidote had had to be rushed in from Alaska at the last minute to save his life? I imagined Mum trying to follow this by reminding Marla, 'Laura nearly got run over by a car today,' and Marla snorting, 'Is that all? You're lucky!'

I sighed. I really envied Oliver. At least he was old enough to eat as much fish – and risk as much death – as he wanted. I longed for the day when I could run out in front of as many cars and spill as much chocolate icing down my front as I liked, without getting all this hassle about it.

I undid the clip I always wear to keep my hair off my face at school and turned my head upside down to brush it. I wondered what was going on downstairs. Usually when Mum and Marla get together they make so much noise talking and laughing I can easily hear them up in my room. Right now I couldn't hear a thing. Was that a good sign or a bad one? What if they were keeping their voices low because they were talking about me?

I decided if they were talking about me I had a right to know what they were saying.

Sure enough, as I put my ear against the living-room door I heard my name.

'Doesn't Laura know the truth?' Marla sounded very serious, not at all her usual self.

'How can I possibly tell her? She's far too young to understand. She'd probably hate me.'

'But you say she's pushing this Guides thing . . .'

I accidentally knocked the door with my foot. The voices inside stopped. I had no choice but to go straight in.

'Here she is.' Marla gave me an exasperated look. 'Honestly, Laura, is the Green Cross Code out of fashion these days or what?'

'It's scaring your mother to death that's in fashion these days,' Mum answered drily. (Like I said, she hates sarcasm, but that doesn't stop her using it herself.)

'I didn't do it on purpose,' I protested.

They sighed and gave me a tell-us-something-else-we've-never-heard-before look. I lost no time in backing out of the room. I hate it when Mum and Marla gang up on me like that. It really makes me wish I wasn't an only child. I'm sure there must be safety in numbers.

47

I waited outside the door to listen. I wanted them to go on with the conversation they'd been having before. What was it that Mum was keeping from me that she thought I was too young to understand? And what had Guides got to do with anything?

They started talking again, but now it was about Marla's son. Apparently he'd spent the whole of his first term's grant in his first three weeks at college. 'He's begging me for a loan, Sylvie. I don't know what to do.'

'Let him starve.'

'Yes, I told him that. But what shall I *do*?'

Bored, I trudged back upstairs. I wished I could find out what was going on. It wasn't like Mum to be this mysterious. She always talked to me, told me things.

I guessed I ought to get on with my homework, or Mum and Marla would start on at me about that as well. Mum's bedroom door was open and I caught sight of the photograph album lying on her bed where I'd left it. She'd told me to put it away, hadn't she? Maybe if she came upstairs and found it flung down on her bed she'd use that as an excuse to stay cross with me too. I knew she kept all the photograph albums in a pile on top of her wardrobe. I dragged her wicker chair across the room and used it to stand on so that I could reach. As I lifted the book upwards I lost my grip and just managed to keep hold of the spine to stop it falling. All the pages splayed out like a fan. A loose piece of paper fluttered out. Impatiently I jumped off the chair and picked it up.

It wasn't a piece of paper. It was a loose photograph that at some time had been ripped down the middle and stuck back together with Sellotape. It was a photo of Mum and her sister that I'd never seen before. They looked sulky, as though they'd just had a fight. I stared at their clothes. Even though the style had changed, the Girl Guide uniforms were unmistakable.

Chapter Six

The next thing that happened is not something I'm exactly proud of. In fact, it's something I nearly made up my mind not to tell you at all, but then I decided that it's sort of essential to what happened afterwards.

The thing is, I got into trouble at school for bullying.

Don't think too horribly of me before I tell you what happened. It's not as though I was going round thumping all the little kids or anything like that.

The trouble was, Janice had started to become friends with another girl in our class, called Helen. Helen went to the same Guides as Janice and I was getting really sick of the two of them going on about the barbecue – or the sausage sizzle as they kept calling it – all the time.

OK, so I know what you're thinking. You're thinking I was jealous. Well, maybe I *was*. Maybe you would have been too. I mean, Janice was *my* best friend and the thought of her doing things with Helen instead of with me didn't exactly thrill me to bits.

'Don't you wish *you* were coming to the sausage sizzle too, Laura?' Helen asked me while we were waiting for Janice to finish fixing her hair. We were standing in front of one of the mirrors in the girls' toilets at school and I was doing my best not to catch a glimpse of myself in it. We'd had swimming that morning and my hair and chlorine just don't have a good relationship.

'Not particularly,' I lied.

'She's not allowed to,' Janice explained, failing to see me scowling at her, because she was concentrating on trying to fix her hairclip.

'Here. I'll do that, Janice.' Helen thumped her schoolbag against my chest for me to hold.

Well, OK, so I haven't exactly *got* a chest yet, but that's beside the point. I let her bag bounce off me and on to the floor (which was still wet from where someone had let one of the sinks overflow).

'Sorry,' I murmured, but I didn't bend down to pick it up.

Helen glared at me. As she bent down to pick up the bag herself, she demanded, 'So why aren't you allowed to go to the sausage sizzle then, Laura? Does your mum think you're too young to be unsupervised around a bonfire or something? Because there'll be lots of grown-up helpers there. Your mum could always ask one of them to sort of babysit you.'

I could feel my face turning beetroot.

'Hey, maybe that *is* why your mum won't let you come, Laura,' Janice giggled. 'Maybe she's worried about the bonfire. I mean, you did nearly set the kitchen on fire that time you tried to dry your shoes under the grill.'

'She did WHAT?!' Helen was gaping at me as if I had a big sign pointing to my brain, saying: *Out of Order*.

'Shut up!' I yelled. 'Of course I'm allowed to go!' I pushed Janice – she'd promised never to tell *anyone* about that time with the shoes – and she slipped on the wet floor. She lost her balance and thudded down on to the ground, banging her head against one of the sinks.

'Janice!' I was horrified.

'FIGHT!' someone shouted, and before I'd even had time to check that Janice was OK, Helen was rushing out to fetch a teacher.

Janice's mum got called up to the school to take Janice home. She wasn't seriously hurt, but she had a slight bump on her head and she said she didn't feel she could cope with maths which was our next – and her least favourite – lesson.

Unfortunately *my* mother got called up to the school as well, only she couldn't come until after four o'clock, by which time nearly everyone else had gone home and I was already halfway through the punishment exercise I'd been set.

'Honestly, Laura, I never had you figured out for a bully!' Mum was on call for the hospital today, which meant it was a particularly bad day for me to get into trouble.

'I'm *not* a bully!' I protested. 'It was an accident!'

'An accident, Laura, is when nobody can be found to be at fault. Pushing someone over does not equal *an accident*!'

'But I didn't push her over. I just pushed her and she *fell* over. It wasn't my fault the floor was slippy.'

I thought we really were going to have an accident on the way home, the way Mum was driving the car.

That night Mum made me phone Janice to apologize. Then she wanted me to hand the phone over to her so that she could apologize to Mrs Bishop (for giving birth to me, I suppose).

'Is your head all right?' I asked Janice timidly.

'You didn't have to go to the doctor or anything, did you?'

'No.'

'I didn't mean you to fall over. I'm really sorry, Janice.'

'So you should be.'

'Oh, come on.' I was getting fed up with grovelling. 'What about the time you pushed me over on the hockey pitch? I had gravel stuck in my knees for ages.'

'Well you shouldn't have told Ewan Spencer that I fancied him, should you?' She lowered her voice. 'Anyway, I wasn't really hurt today. I had a really nice afternoon at home watching TV.' She spoke louder again. 'Helen phoned tonight to see how I was. Listen, we need to know for definite about the sausage sizzle. Did you mean it when you said you were allowed to go? Because we've got to have cooking partners and if you're not coming I've said I'll be Helen's partner. I know you don't like Helen, but she is my best friend at Guides—'

'I *am* coming,' I interrupted hotly. 'Mum hasn't actually said I can yet but I know I can get her to change her mind. I just have to pick the right time to ask her.'

'Are you sure?' Janice sounded sceptical.

'Laura?' Mum stuck her head round the door.

'Look, I've got to go. My mum wants to speak to your mum. Promise you'll be my partner and not Helen's?'

'OK. But you've got to promise you'll definitely come. If you don't come and I get left without any partner at all . . .' She didn't finish the sentence but she didn't need to. I know a threat when I hear one.

Chapter Seven

You're probably not as daft as I am so you probably won't need this piece of advice. I'm going to give it to you anyway though, just in case.

Never, ever, if you're trying to get your mum to change her mind about something, ask your divorced father to speak to her on your behalf.

'Who the hell does he think he is, telling me how to bring up my own daughter!' Mum smashed the telephone receiver down, making Rory leap out of his chair and rush for the cat flap. I started to back out of the room slowly. I was pretty sure there was worse to come, especially as Mum was on call for the hospital again today, which meant she couldn't have the gin and tonic she usually prepared in advance if ever she had to speak to Dad on the phone.

'Well, she is his daughter too,' Hamish said, looking up from the Sunday paper.

I stopped in my tracks. My mouth dropped open. Did Hamish have a death wish or what? I glanced nervously at Mum. She was staring at Hamish as though he'd just changed from a handsome prince into a particularly ugly frog.

I got out of that room as fast as I could. In my mind's eye I could already see the blood and guts splattered across the walls. Hamish wouldn't stand a chance.

I sat on my bedroom floor waiting for the shouting to begin. This was all my fault. If I hadn't asked Dad to ask Mum to let me go to Guides, none of this would be happening. I must have been crazy to think that getting Dad on my side would help. Getting Dad on my side was the worst thing I could possibly have done. My case was doomed for ever now, and Hamish was doomed too into the bargain. The really strange thing was that I didn't feel that great about getting rid of Hamish like this. I just felt guilty. I nervously picked at the fluff on my carpet, wishing they'd get on with their row. I wanted it over and done with. I was sick of sitting here holding in my breath. It reminded me of when Dad lived with us, except that there were never any delays in kick-off before one of Mum and Dad's yelling matches. With them, you ran for cover the minute you realized the two of them were in the same room at the same time.

I shuffled across the floor to my CD player,

pressed the Play button and fished my wooden swords out from under my bed. The good thing about Highland Dancing is that you have to count the steps. Counting stops you thinking about anything else.

'Laura, I'm going out.'

I jumped. Mum was standing in my doorway, pulling the belt tight on her raincoat. She looked quite calm.

'I've a patient to go and see. I shan't be long.'

I bent down and put the CD on Pause. 'Shall I go over to Janice's?' I started to hunt for my shoes.

'Come on, Laura.' Mum sounded exasperated. 'Surely you know Hamish well enough now for me to leave you on your own with him for an hour.'

'But I thought . . .' I was imagining Hamish either kicked out on to the street or lying on the living room floor ready for burial after dark in our back garden.

'And, Laura, I'm sorry for what I said about your father just now. Hamish is right. It's not fair on you for me to react like that. Of course Dad will always be interested in how I'm bringing you up. You're his daughter. He cares about you.' She pulled her gloves out of her pocket. 'Now I must dash. I'll see you in a bit.'

I stared after her, utterly flabbergasted. What had Hamish done? Hypnotized her?

Ten minutes later I was still sitting on my bed staring dumbly at the pattern my swords made on the floor. For some reason it didn't surprise me when Hamish appeared in my bedroom doorway, a packet of chocolate digestives in one hand and a can of Irn-Bru in the other. Mum has a nostalgic attachment to Irn-Bru because it's made in Scotland, so I'm allowed to drink it even though it rots my teeth.

'Voila!' Hamish presented the can on the palm of his hand like a waiter presenting a bottle of wine in a restaurant.

I had to force myself not to laugh. I do find Hamish funny sometimes, however hard I try not to.

'*Merci*,' I replied. If Hamish thought I was going to be impressed just because he knew a bit of French, he was sorely mistaken. I'd been learning French myself at school for nearly a year now.

'That's a seriously good French accent.'

I narrowed my eyes. 'At our last parents' night my French teacher said I had one of the worst accents in my class,' I said gruffly.

His eyes sparkled. 'Really? All the other people

in your class must have exceptionally good accents then.' I noticed for the first time that he had quite nice eyes. They were dark brown and warm-looking.

I watched him unpick the end of the chocolate digestive packet. 'Did Mum say you could have those?' I demanded.

He pulled a face in mock horror. 'I didn't ask. Are you going to tell on me?'

I felt myself go pink. He was being too smart now. I couldn't think why Mum liked him. She hates people who are too smart. 'I don't want one,' I snapped as he offered me the packet.

'What? After all that dancing? You'll have to keep your blood-sugar levels up, you know, if you want to stay the course. Scottish Highland Dancing is all about stamina. And I should know.'

It took a great deal of mental energy not to give him the satisfaction of asking how he knew, especially as I'm a curious person by nature. I watched him devour half a biscuit in one bite, thinking it would serve him right if he choked on it and that if he did I'd wait for him to go blue before I thumped his back.

He didn't seem to care whether I was interested in what he had to say or not. 'Laura, you are speaking to the six-times gold medallist in the Kilmalochry children's Highland Dance champion-ships. Have you got some music there?' He bent down to untie his shoelaces, kicked off his shoes to reveal a pair of bright red holey socks, and switched on my CD. 'Now I was never too hot at the sword dance, always afraid I'd stub my toe on the swords. How about a demonstration Highland Fling instead?'

He launched into the most chaotic Highland Fling I've ever seen, jigging about wildly and making up the steps he couldn't remember, which looked to me to be just about all of them.

It was far too painful to watch. 'You're doing it all wrong!' I kicked the swords out of the way and stood with my heels together, both feet pointing outwards, my back arched, both fists on my waist, waiting for a suitable bit in the music to start off. Then I was jigging away alongside Hamish, shriek-ing at him every time he bumped into me. 'Your feet are all wrong! It's like this! Watch!' And that's how I came to be giving Hamish a refresher course in Highland Dancing when Mum arrived back from the hospital.

'Kilmalochry's Gold Medallist is about to make a comeback,' Hamish greeted her.

Mum stood for a long time watching us, smiling.

Hamish was panting as we sat on the floor putting on our shoes after Mum went downstairs to make dinner. His face was pink and he suddenly seemed a lot younger than before. I really wanted to know how old he was, so I asked him.

He looked up, pushing his fringe out of his eyes. 'I'm thirty-two.'

'Really?' I found this interesting. 'Does Mum know you're younger than her?'

He looked puzzled. 'But your mum's—'

'Thirty-five, which makes you three years younger than her.'

'Do you people want soup?' Mum called up the stairs.

Hamish was starting to smile.

I stared at him. 'What?'

'You're a gem, Laura. A gem!' He was chuckling now.

'You're mad,' I said.

Mum had come upstairs to find out what was going on. 'Do you want soup or not?' She looked a little nervously at Hamish, who was still laughing. 'Did I miss something here?'

'Nothing at all!' Hamish leaped up, put his arm round her waist and kissed her cheek. 'Now did I hear the word soup? That wouldn't be home-made lentil soup just like my mother used to make, would it?'

'No it wouldn't,' Mum answered sweetly. 'But I've got some lentils in the cupboard if you want to make some.'

'My granny in Scotland makes really good lentil soup,' I chipped in. 'And when Mum was a wee girl she didn't like it so she used to spoon lots of hers into Kathleen's bowl when nobody was looking.' Granny had told me that the last time we visited. Very, very occasionally Granny will mention Kathleen in some neutral sort of way like that, but even then her voice shakes slightly and she'll glance across at Kathleen's photo on the mantelpiece as though she's still longing for her to walk back in through the door. I looked up at Hamish. 'Do you know about Kathleen? She was Mum's little sister. She would've been my auntie if she hadn't died. I haven't got any aunties because my dad is an only child and so is Mum now.'

'Laura, we're going to eat in a minute,' Mum interrupted briskly. 'Come and help me set the table.'

Mum was in a good mood all through dinner. She's usually a bit tense when she's on call, but tonight Hamish was making her laugh a lot. He was making me laugh a lot too. I had to keep reminding myself that I didn't like him, which got more and more difficult as he kept paying me as much attention as he was paying Mum, refilling my empty glass (with orange juice) and listening to me as if I was saying something interesting when most of the time I wasn't. He even got Mum to let me have a second helping of ice cream by pointing out that I'd only had a very small portion the first time.

It was while Mum was in the kitchen making coffee that I had my brainwave. Getting Dad to speak up for me hadn't worked, but maybe getting Hamish on my side would.

'Hamish,' I began cautiously, 'were you ever in the Boy Scouts?'

Mum came through from the kitchen.

'The Scouts?' Hamish grinned. 'Now it's funny you should ask that because I was actually expelled from the Scouts.' His grin widened. 'I caused a can of baked beans to explode at our annual sausage sizzle.'

I giggled. Mum smiled as well, until I continued, looking at her pointedly, 'You were *allowed* to go to the sausage sizzle, then?'

Mum began to gather up our plates noisily.

'Oh yes. Until the famous baked-bean incident.'

'So your parents *let* you go to Scouts?'

'Let me go? They practically forced me. They thought it would be character-building!'

'That's what my friend Janice says about Guides, that it's character-building. She says it teaches you how to do all sorts of things.'

'Laura, help me clear the table,' Mum interrupted sharply.

'Hamish, if I really wanted to go to Guides, you'd let me, wouldn't you? You wouldn't *ban* me from going?'

'LAURA!' Mum bellowed.

Hamish got more of a fright than I did. He stared at my mother as if he thought she'd gone loopy.

'I'm sorry, Hamish, but Laura already knows my views on this.' Mum's voice was shaking. A red rash had come out on her neck. She was fixing me with a look that warned me not to open my mouth again for at least the next ten hours.

I was too angry to stay quiet. 'It's not fair! Granny let *you* go to Guides! Just because you didn't like it doesn't mean I won't! I wish I lived with Dad! *He'd* let me go!' I leaped up and ran out of the room.

Up in my bedroom I burst into tears. 'I'm going to join the Guides, I'm going to, I'm going to, I'm going to,' I sobbed angrily. I flung myself down on the floor, scrambling under the bed to find my diary. Mum is always going on about how good it is to keep a diary and how glad she was that she'd kept one while she was growing up. I'd managed to keep mine for three weeks this year before I got fed up with it. Now I only ever wrote in it when I was really excited or really angry.

'I HATE MUM!' I scrawled in huge thick letters right across the page.

I'd hidden the photo of Mum and Kathleen in the back of the diary. As I peered again at Kathleen's sad little face, I whispered, 'No wonder you look so miserable, having *her* for your sister.'

Voices were being raised downstairs. I strained to listen. I couldn't hear properly so I crept out on to the landing.

'I just don't understand you! I've been trying really hard all day and just when I'm starting to get somewhere—' Hamish sounded really exasperated.

'I can't let her get away with answering me back like that.'

'Sure, but why all the fuss in the first place? Was I paying her too much attention? Were you feeling left out?'

'Don't be ridiculous! I want you to pay her lots of attention. It's not that!' There was a long pause. 'She's been going on at me for weeks to let her go to Guides.'

'So why don't you let her? What's the big deal?'

'It's not as simple as that!'

Their voices were getting quieter. I had to go to the bottom of the stairs to hear properly.

'I never want her to go to Guides. I never want to see her in one of those uniforms.' Mum's voice was going funny. 'I'm sorry, Hamish. You must think I'm being stupid, but I just can't be rational about it.' She made a strange little choking noise.

'Sylvie . . .' Hamish's voice was suddenly softer. 'What is it?'

She sniffed. 'There's something else, something that happened when I was in Guides. It's to do with my sister.' She sniffed again. 'Oh, God, I suppose you've got a right to know . . .'

They shut the living-room door. I crept across the hall and pressed my ear against the door. I could just make out their voices. I heard Mum whisper, 'Wait a minute.' Then they put on some music and I couldn't hear a word.

Fuming, I ran back upstairs. I picked up the photograph again, staring at it. What had happened when Mum and Kathleen were at Guides? What did Hamish have a right to know that I didn't?

Still clutching the photo, I went to fetch my magnifying glass. Dad had sent me it for my last birthday, after I'd told him I wanted to be a detective when I grew up. (I love my magnifying glass. It's not a toy one. It's just like the ones real detectives have.)

Carefully I inspected the photograph again, searching for some sort of clue. Kathleen was sweet and pretty-looking. Her hair was tied back with a ribbon. Mum was standing awkwardly and her hair looked like it hadn't been brushed for a week. I scrutinized their faces. Neither of them was smiling but I saw now that their expressions were quite different. Mum looked sullen and angry. Kathleen, standing at her side, looked scared.

Chapter Eight

'Why do you think Kathleen looks so frightened?' I asked Janice, showing her the photograph under the magnifying glass.

Janice peered at the photo for a long time. We were at her house. Her mum had sent us upstairs for Janice to get changed ready for Guides. 'Maybe she was scared of cameras. Some people are scared of telephones. My little sister runs a mile whenever it rings.'

'She doesn't look scared in all the other photos of her. It's just in this one where they're in their Guide uniforms.'

'Have you asked your mum about it?' She pulled the hairband out of her hair and started to brush it.

'I keep telling you, every time you mention Guides to Mum she just about has a fit. Something happened to her at Guides that she won't tell me. It's to do with Kathleen but I don't know what. I don't know how to find out either.'

Janice looked at me sharply. 'She *is* going to let you join, isn't she?'

'Of course,' I replied, avoiding looking at her. 'I

just haven't found the right time to ask her yet. Here. Let me do that.'

I love putting Janice's hair in a plait. I'm thinking about being a hairdresser when I grow up. Mum doesn't seem particularly against the idea although she isn't as enthusiastic as when I wanted to be a detective.

'Why don't you ask her if you can come to Guides with me tonight? We're allowed to take guests.'

'I can't. Mum's taking me to some boring concert thing tonight.'

Janice pulled a face. 'Is Hamish going with you?'

'Yes.' I was concentrating hard on finishing the plait. 'Pass me the hairband, will you?'

'Do you think they're going to get married?'

My fingers slipped and the whole plait unravelled. I stared at it. I felt really strange. 'Who knows?' I answered, trying to sound normal. Sometimes when you try to keep sounding normal you start feeling normal pretty quickly again too.

'What's wrong?'

'Nothing.' I glared at myself in the mirror. 'Look at my hair! I hate it! I look like a scarecrow!' I grabbed a clump of my hair and yanked it so that it hurt. I started to speak very rapidly. 'The minute

I'm old enough I'm going to get one of those perms that make your hair go straight. I'd get one now only Mum won't let me. She says lots of people would give their eye teeth to have naturally curly hair. She doesn't understand. Not like Dad.' I could see Dad now, pulling me down to sit on his lap so that Mum could attack my hair with a hairbrush, joking that he'd had hair just like mine when he was young and he'd been really glad when he started going bald at thirty.

I clamped my teeth together very tightly. Sometimes I feel like Dad's right inside me. Then I have to tell myself that he's not really here at all. Then I feel so empty it hurts.

Janice was looking anxious. 'I know,' she gasped, rushing over to her wardrobe, 'let's see what you look like as a Guide.' She practically threw her uniform at me.

'Come on, it doesn't look that bad!' she protested after I'd put on the uniform and was standing in front of the mirror, screwing up my face. I was just about to answer that I thought it did, when Janice's mum stuck her head round the door, carrying a tray of orange juice and biscuits. I really love the way Mrs Bishop always makes a fuss of us like that. I said that to Mum once, hoping she'd take the hint, and she said that if I ever lost the use of my legs she promised to bring trays of juice and biscuits upstairs to me too.

'What do you think of Laura?' Janice asked.

'Very smart.' Mrs Bishop put the tray down on the floor, catching sight of the photograph of Mum and Kathleen, picking it up before I could stop her. 'Who's this? Is it your mum?'

I desperately wanted to snatch it out of her hand and hide it behind my back. It took a huge amount of effort just to stand there and nod.

'And who's this standing beside her?'

The doorbell rang.

I stared at Janice in alarm. Mum never usually got back this early. I started to struggle out of the uniform, frantically signalling to Janice to do something.

Janice rushed to block the doorway. 'Mum, you musn't tell Doctor Rorison about the photo. It's a secret. She doesn't know Laura found it. She gets upset when anyone mentions Kathleen, so you musn't say anything, OK?'

'Who *is* Kathleen?' Mrs Bishop strode across the room and pulled the uniform up over my head for me. 'What is all this about? You shouldn't have secrets from your mother, Laura.'

Me having secrets from *Mum*? That had to be the biggest joke I'd ever heard. 'Please,' I begged. 'Don't say anything to Mum.' But I knew it was no good. Mrs Bishop was a mother and Mum was a mother, which meant that they were both on the same side. Mum was going to kill me when she found out I'd taken her photograph. She was probably going to hate me forever.

The bell rang again.

'Janice, let me past,' her mother ordered.

'Mum, the secret's to do with Christmas,' Janice gasped. 'It's to do with a present Laura's giving her mum for Christmas. It was your granny's idea about the photo, wasn't it, Laura? They're getting it framed for her mum for Christmas. If you say anything you'll spoil the surprise.'

'Christmas?' Mrs Bishop frowned. 'That's a long way away, isn't it?'

'Yes, but Laura's got to send the photo to her granny and then her granny's got to find someone to frame it and—'

'All right, all right. But make sure you take care of that photograph, Laura. I'm sure it's very precious to your mother.' She rushed downstairs to answer the door.

'So precious she tore it up and it had to be stuck

73

back together with Sellotape,' I muttered, button-
ing up my blouse as fast as I could. I flopped down
on the bed. 'Phew! I thought I was done for!'

Janice was looking thoughtful. 'Maybe it wasn't
your mum who tore up the photo. Maybe it was
someone else.'

'Like who?'

Janice shrugged. 'Kathleen?'

I stared at my friend. I hadn't thought of that.

'LAURA!' Mum was yelling up the stairs.

Quickly I gathered up the rest of my things.
'Thanks, Janice,' I murmured shyly. 'For saying all
that to your mum. I'd never have thought up anything as good as that.'

Janice grinned. She's pretty proud of her expert-
ise at lying to her mother. 'Here. Don't forget this.'
She handed me the photograph. She giggled. 'This
is really exciting. It's like being in a mystery story
or something.'

As I ran downstairs to join Mum I felt really
pleased that I'd told the whole thing to Janice. At
least I wasn't in this on my own any more.

As soon as we got in Mum went straight up to
her room to phone Hamish. She said she wanted to
check what time he was picking us up that night.
Theoretically that ought to take two minutes, but

knowing Mum and Hamish when they get on the phone I figured it was more likely to take two hours.

'I'd much rather be going to Guides than some boring old concert,' I complained loudly to Rory, stroking his tummy as he lay stretched out on the kitchen floor.

There was a loud rapping on the front door and the sound of the letter box being rattled. I jumped up.

'Who is it?' I shouted. Since Dad moved out, Mum's been really strict about always asking who it is before you open the door. It was Marla who taught her to do that after she'd forgotten herself and ended up having her ex-husband barging in demanding she put him up for the night because his new girlfriend had locked him out. 'You never know what undesirable character might turn up on your doorstep,' Marla was always saying. 'A woman on her own just can't be too careful.'

A hand with long red fingernails appeared through the letter box. 'When are you going to get this bell fixed?'

I only knew one person with nails like that. I undid the latch on the door and opened it. 'Mum's upstairs on the phone,' I said, staring at Marla's hat. Marla always wears hats. This one was black and squashed-looking with a brooch pinned at the front.

'A-ha! To this man of hers, I hope?'

'Hamish,' I replied flatly.

She followed me into the living room, dumping her coat on the settee and removing her hat. 'Don't you like him?'

I shrugged. 'I suppose so.' I picked up the hat and tried it on. I like hats. They hide your hair.

'You suppose you like him or you suppose you don't?' She led the way through to the kitchen without waiting for an answer. 'I thought I'd pop in on my way home from work to see how things were. I hardly ever seem to see your mother these days.'

'That's Hamish's fault,' I said, watching her fill the kettle.

'Well, that's what I was hoping. She seems very happy with him. I haven't met him yet. What's he like?'

It's odd when somebody asks you what somebody is like and you realize you don't really know, even though you've spent weeks with them constantly in and out of your house. I thought Marla would think I was being difficult if I said that, so I made a huge effort to describe Hamish. 'He's tall

76

with brown eyes and brown hair and he's Scottish. When he was a wee boy he won his local Highland Dancing championships six years in a row, but I think he might be making that up. And he's younger than Mum. He's only thirty-two.'

Marla was reaching inside the fridge for the milk, so I couldn't see her face. 'And is he nice to you?'

I thought about it. 'I suppose so.'

'But you don't like him?'

I blushed. 'I didn't say I didn't *like* him exactly . . .'

'I see.' She tossed a teabag into a mug and smiled at me. 'So what have you been up to lately? Any new boyfriends?'

'There aren't even any *old* boyfriends,' I protested indignantly. Marla always teases me about boys.

She laughed. 'How about showing me where you've hidden the chocolate biscuits?'

We went through to sit down in the living room. 'Is she likely to spend all night on the phone to him, do you think?'

'She can't, because we've got to go out tonight.' I pulled a face. 'It's a concert at the Symphony Hall.'

'Really? That's very good. Oliver would never have gone to anything like that at your age. If it wasn't in the charts then he didn't want to know.'

I was about to reply that I didn't really want to know either when I had the brainwave (my second one). Getting Dad on my side hadn't worked. Getting Hamish on my side hadn't worked. But Mum always listened to Marla, didn't she?

'Marla, did Oliver go to Scouts when he was my age?'

She blew on her tea. 'I don't think so. Oh yes, I remember now. He went along because a friend of his was going, and then decided he didn't like it. Why?'

'I want to join the Guides but Mum won't let me.'

Her expression instantly changed. She eyed me warily. 'Oh yes?' She took a large gulp of tea, wincing as it burned her mouth.

'Do you think that's fair?'

'Well . . .' Marla, who has got to be the most unsquirmable person in the world, was visibly squirming.

'You let Oliver go to Scouts, didn't you? So if I was your daughter, would you let me go to Guides?'

'Laura, where is your mother?'

78

'I told you! Upstairs on the—'

'Marla!' Mum burst into the room in her dressing gown, her old blue towelling one, the one she only wears when Hamish isn't around. 'I thought I heard voices down here. Listen, I'm really sorry I haven't phoned you. How are you? How's Oliver? I was just about to jump in the shower. Hamish is taking us to the Symphony Hall tonight. Did Laura tell you?' She paused as she glanced from Marla's face to mine. 'What is it?'

Marla started to speak but I interrupted. 'Oliver was allowed to go to Scouts, so why won't you let me go to Guides? It's not fair!' I stood up. 'Mrs Bishop says people should be allowed to try things out for themselves!'

Mum gritted her teeth. 'Laura, I've told you my reasons.' She sounded like she was fighting to stay calm, but I didn't care whether she stayed calm or not any more. I just wanted the truth.

'No you haven't! Not the *real* reason!'

Her voice was low and unsteady as she demanded, 'What do you mean?'

I couldn't stand all the pretending any longer. 'I know the real reason you won't let me go!' I shouted. 'It's because of Kathleen!'

Chapter Nine

'Sylvie, calm down. Laura, go upstairs. Go on.'

Marla sounded just like one of my teachers breaking up a fight in the school playground.

I slunk out from behind Marla's back, giving Mum a wide berth as I fled the room. I didn't even let myself think what might have happened if Marla hadn't been there to jump in between us. This story would have ended right here, probably, with me being carted off in a coffin, and you never getting to hear what had happened to Kathleen.

I shut the door behind me and waited outside to listen. I got ready to run if one of them came out to check. I pretty much expected Mum to check, since she knows what I'm like for listening behind doors.

'How can she know? How can she know? It's Jack! I bet it's Jack, the . . . !' (Jack is my dad. I won't actually write down the string of words Mum used at this point to describe him, because I want you to be allowed to read this book and I know Mum wouldn't let ME read a book that had words like that in it.)

'But why would Jack tell her?'

'Because he's a—!'

'True, but he's still hardly likely to tell her something like that, is he? What could he possibly have to gain?'

'I don't know.' There was a slight pause, then Mum burst out, 'Oh my God, you don't think he wants custody of her, do you? You don't think he's trying to turn her against me? What if he took me to court? What if they brought up all that stuff about Kathleen in court?'

'Sylvie, stop it. Why should Jack want custody of her? He hardly ever phones her. He even forgot her birthday this year and you had to go and buy that magnifying glass and pretend it was from him. Sylvie, he's just not interested enough in her to—'

I burst into the room. I was shaking with rage. I glared at Marla, hating her, hating her more than I'd ever hated anyone, screaming, 'I hate you! I hate you!' until my voice gave up and all I could hear was myself sobbing.

'Laura!' Mum came rushing over, making to grab me into her arms but I shook her off savagely.

'I hate that magnifying glass! I should've known you'd bought it! It was a stupid present! Dad would never buy me anything that stupid!' I kicked out at her.

'Laura—'

I turned and ran upstairs to the bathroom which is the only room in our house with a door you can lock.

I sat on the floor, leaning against the bath, crying. So what if Dad hadn't bought me the magnifying glass? That didn't mean anything. Anyone could forget a birthday. It didn't mean he wasn't interested in me. The only reason he didn't phone me very much was because I could never wait as long as him so I nearly always ended up phoning him first. It was true that he hardly ever answered any of the emails I sent him but that was because he was really bad at checking his emails – Mum had told me that herself, hadn't she? – and besides, he was always really busy. Mum won't let me go to Australia on my own yet. And the only reason Dad hadn't wanted to come and visit *me* this summer was because he couldn't leave his wife on her own with their new baby. It's a very exhausting business looking after a baby. Everyone knows that.

'Laura, baby, please open this door.'

I grabbed a towel off the rack and buried my face in it.

'Laura, let me in.' She rattled the door handle.

'I want to be on my own,' I sniffed. Sometimes that works with Mum, sometimes it doesn't.

'Laura, if you don't open this door immediately I'm going to force it open and you can pay for anything that breaks in the process.'

I slowly stood up. She sounded quite calm, though whether that meant it was safe to come out or not I just didn't know any more. What I did know was that Mum rarely makes threats that she doesn't intend to keep. She was quite capable of breaking down the door with a sledgehammer just to stop me getting the better of her.

I pulled back the lock.

We stood staring at each other. I don't know what my face looked like but it couldn't have been any worse than hers. Her eyes were red and puffy with black circles underneath and her skin was all blotchy.

'You shouldn't listen behind doors, Laura, especially not after you've just left a room. If you keep doing it you're going to have a very unpleasant life.'

'Well, people shouldn't say horrid things about other people behind their backs!' I replied angrily.

She grabbed hold of my arm. 'Laura, what you heard Marla say about your father just now, you've got to remember that she only sees things from my side, because she's my friend. She said those things to try and make me feel better. Sometimes people say things to try and make other people feel better that aren't exactly true.' She frowned. 'It's true Daddy forgot your birthday, but I'm sure he'd have remembered himself and sent you a belated present if I hadn't got angry and gone out and bought you a present from him myself. I was probably wrong to do that. I expect you'd have preferred a belated present that was really from him, wouldn't you?'

I wanted to answer but I couldn't. I was starting to cry again.

Mum flung her arms round me. She held me really tightly. A few minutes ago, when I'd been crying on my own in the bathroom, I'd been too scared to cry this hard.

She kissed the top of my head. 'Daddy loves you very much and so do I,' she said firmly.

'I don't want to go and live with Dad,' I craned my neck to look up at her. 'I won't ever have to, will I?'

She looked fierce. 'Of course not!'

On our way back downstairs she stopped suddenly and grabbed my hand. 'Laura, what did you mean just now –' she cleared her throat – 'about Kathleen?'

I froze. This was it. At long last, here was my chance to find out what had happened. 'I know there was an accident,' I murmured shakily. 'And I know that's why you won't let me go to Guides. And I found that photo of you and Kathleen in your Guide uniforms, the one that was torn up. What happened, Mum? How did Kathleen die?'

'You found that photograph?' She swallowed. She looked very pale. 'Your father didn't tell you anything?'

I shook my head, waiting.

She was staring straight ahead, gazing at nothing. 'Kathleen died while we were at Guides. It was an accident. That's all there is to tell.'

'What sort of accident?'

'Laura, I'm not going to give you all the gory details because it's too painful. If you can't understand that—'

'I'm sorry,' I gasped. I felt bad. I almost started crying all over again.

Mum looked like she felt like crying too.

We both just stood there.

I desperately wanted to ask her something else, but I was scared she'd be angry with me again.

Very, very nervously, I whispered, 'Mum, what was Kathleen like?'

At first I thought she wasn't going to answer. Then she gave a funny little half-smile. 'She was very pretty and very confident and everybody liked her much better than they liked me.' She laughed shortly. 'I was so jealous I used to pick fights with her all the time.'

'You looked like you'd just had a fight in that photograph.'

She didn't say anything.

'Who tore it up? I think it was you, but Janice thinks it might've been Kathleen.'

Her grip on my hand tightened. 'You showed the photograph to Janice?'

'Mum, you're hurting.' I pulled my hand away sharply. What was wrong with her?

'Laura, look, I'm sorry.' She had gone even paler. 'I just don't want the whole street knowing our business, OK?'

'Janice isn't the whole street,' I protested sulkily. 'Anyway, the other day you said they could gossip all they liked.'

'About Hamish. Not about this.'

'But who did tear up the photo?' I persisted stubbornly.

From the look in her eyes I was pretty sure she was remembering either tearing it up herself or standing watching someone else tear it up in front of her. 'I really can't remember,' she answered without looking at me.

I didn't believe her.

Chapter Ten

When Marla finally gave up trying to make friends with me and left, Mum noticed the time and panicked. 'Hamish will be here in half an hour. Have you got anything to wear that doesn't need ironing?'

Mum hates ironing and she generally waits until both our wardrobes are empty before she does any. When Dad was here, he used to iron more of our clothes than she did. Mum and Granny had a huge row about that last time we went up to Scotland. Mum was going on about how women who iron their husband's shirts are letting down the whole of womankind, and Granny had snorted, 'Well, dear, perhaps if you'd ironed a few more of Jack's shirts he might not have rushed off quite so quickly to Australia.' Granny is pretty good at saying things that make Mum mad, but I'd never seen Mum get quite as mad as she did then.

'The only thing is Granny's red dress,' I said, pulling a face. 'But I can iron something myself.'

'I haven't got time to show you how to use the iron just now, Laura,' she answered impatiently.

'You don't have to. Mrs Bishop already showed me. It's easy!'

She didn't look as pleased as I'd expected. 'How wonderful of Mrs Bishop,' she muttered in the sort of voice people use when they're saying the opposite of what they really mean. 'Just wear the red dress.' She banged my door shut.

I stared after her, flabbergasted. Granny had knitted me the horrible red woollen dress for my last birthday, and so far I'd only ever worn it twice: once so that Mum could take a photo of me in it to send back to Granny and once to cheer Marla up after she split from the only boyfriend she's had since she got divorced – when she saw me in that dress she immediately stopped crying and started laughing.

I decided Mum couldn't be serious. I waited until I heard her go into the bathroom, then I tip-toed downstairs.

Our ironing board stands permanently in our back room so that Mum can emergency-iron whatever she wants to wear five minutes before she goes out the door. I sifted through the various heaps of clothes on all the chairs – there's never space to actually sit down in that room – until I found my favourite dress. It's a greeny-blue one that Mum bought for me in the sales and I love it. I look really grown-up in it, in fact Mum nearly took it back to the shop after I first tried it on because she said I looked too grown-up. If it hadn't been for Marla laughing at her and saying, 'Well, she *is* growing up,' I'd probably never have got to keep it. Marla's really good at sticking up for me when Mum gets in one of her flaps. I felt a bit guilty thinking about the horrible glare I'd given Marla as she walked out the door tonight. It was just that how could I be friends with her again after what she'd said about Dad?

I'd just finished ironing when I heard a knocking on our front door and the flap on the letter box being rattled. Hamish always makes a lot of noise when he arrives at the door, as if he thinks Mum and me are deaf or something. I suppose I can't really blame him considering how long it always takes for either of us to let him in. Mum's always upstairs having a last-minute panic about whether she looks fat in whatever it is she's wearing, and I'm always reluctant to go to the door straight away in case Hamish thinks I've decided to like him. I looked at my watch. He was dead on time as usual. That was another reason I couldn't under-stand why Mum liked him so much. Normally she gets really irritated by people being too punctual. She says it makes her nervous because she never manages to be on time for anything herself. I let him rattle the letter box for a bit longer while I carefully switched off and unplugged the iron. (Mrs Bishop says it's dangerous to leave an iron plugged in, even if you're only going to be away for a minute.)

He greeted me with a much bigger smile than I'd have greeted anyone who'd kept me standing on the doorstep for all that time. 'This street has got to have the twitchiest net curtains in the whole of Birmingham,' he said, lifting his arm to wave at Mrs Smart, next-door-but-one to Janice, who Mum says is a much better deterrent to burglars than all the Neighbourhood Watch stickers and burglar alarms in our street put together.

Mortified, I dragged him in off the doorstep by the sleeve of his jacket. I'd thought Mum was bad for embarrassing me in public. I stared at his tie. 'Can't you wear a normal tie?' I demanded huffily, thinking how typical it was of him to have to wear a bright purple bow tie. 'That looks really silly.'

'I think it looks very distinguished,' Mum pronounced from the top of the stairs, using that special tone of voice that she only ever uses with

Hamish, the one that seems to come right from the back of her throat. She was smiling into his eyes as she came down the stairs, and he was smiling right back at her. I felt really shut out.

'I'm wearing this, OK?' I thrust the green dress in front of Mum's face defiantly.

'That's lovely, darling.' She pushed it out of her way so that her view of Hamish and his horrible bow tie remained unobstructed.

'I ironed it myself,' I added loudly. 'I didn't want to wear the red one.'

Before Mum could answer, Hamish reached out and gently laid his hand on top of my head. 'Honey, how about getting changed? Otherwise we're going to be late and they won't let us into the concert.'

I stared at him. The way he'd said 'Honey' gave me a shivery sort of feeling inside. Dad used to call me 'Sweetheart' in just that same tone of voice, as if I really mattered to him. I went upstairs feeling confused. Why couldn't everything just be straightforward like it was when I was little? I never had to worry then about whether people meant what they said or not, and I'd never have dreamt in a million years that my dad could change his mind about being my dad and zoom off to be somebody else's in Australia.

I was really glad to be wearing my green dress and not my red one as I sat between Mum and Hamish in the Birmingham Symphony Hall that night waiting for the conductor (who I'd never heard of but Mum said is a really well-known man) to join the orchestra on the stage. I'd never been in the Symphony Hall before and unless you live in Birmingham, with a mother who thinks exposure to classical music is essential to your development and who threatens never to let you listen to any pop music again unless you go with her, you probably haven't either. I don't really know how to describe it except that it's really huge, with rows and rows of red seats on four different levels. We were sitting at the highest level at the front, which meant we were much nearer to the ceiling than we were to the stage. The ceiling was made up of lots of impressive-looking speakers and things which Hamish tried to tell me were all connected up to an alarm system which went off if anyone in the orchestra played a wrong note. 'It's called Quality Control,' he grinned, which made Mum start laughing.

'There isn't anybody else my age here at all,' I hissed angrily at my mother. It always annoys me when Mum and Hamish start laughing at a joke I don't think is all that funny, especially when I'm not feeling the least bit like laughing myself.

'Not all children are as lucky as you, Laura.'

I scowled, sliding down in my seat and placing my feet on the back of the seat in front. Mum rolled up her programme and whacked me across the ankles with it. I dropped my feet to the floor, glaring at her.

'Have you ever been to a classical concert before?' Hamish asked me.

I shook my head sulkily.

'Ah well, the trick, you see, is to clear your throat in all the right places. Isn't that right, Sylvie?'

Mum laughed again, which really irritated me.

The audience started clapping as the conductor walked on stage and bowed, and however hard I tried not to, I couldn't help liking him immediately. His hair was even messier than mine.

'They're starting with Pachelbel's Canon,' Mum whispered excitedly. 'I love this piece.'

I sighed loudly. 'Have you brought any sweets?'

'Shush!'

The main part of the concert was something I vaguely recognized the beginning of, which probably meant Mum had the CD at home. I usually recognize the first thirty seconds of all Mum's classical music because that's how long it takes me to escape from the room whenever she puts some on.

Unfortunately, there was no escaping the room tonight. The music seemed to go on for ever and I started to think that maybe it really was possible to die of boredom.

'Remember I want to be cremated, not buried,' I hissed at Mum.

She ignored me.

I decided I had to take action. I started by counting all the people in the orchestra, followed by all the people in the first row of the audience, then the second row, then the third. I scanned the whole of the stalls looking for other children and couldn't spot any at all. No wonder. They were probably all at home watching TV with their babysitters. I thought longingly of Cheryl and decided I was never going to be horrible to her ever again, not even when she nagged at me to go to bed on time. I started to fidget. I couldn't see how anyone could manage to sit still in here for more than five minutes, even with their mother giving them the sort of I'm-warning-you look Mum was giving me right then. I peered at my watch. I started to *want* to die of boredom. At least that way I wouldn't have to sit through the rest of the concert.

It was Hamish who came to my rescue next time there was a pause. (A pause is what you call it when the orchestra finishes playing and everyone starts clearing their throats and coughing and you think it's the interval and you're just deciding what sort of ice cream you want when they start up again.) Hamish made such an exaggerated, funny noise clearing his throat that I started to giggle. It was really hard to stop after the music started again, because Hamish kept pulling faces at me when Mum wasn't looking that made me want to giggle all the more. I could tell Mum was getting more and more cross, so I did try to stop, but I've got to admit that having Hamish as my partner in crime made me feel too safe to bother trying very hard.

Hamish was still pulling faces at me in the driving mirror in the car on the way home. I thought Mum might be in a bad mood with me, but she didn't seem to be. She sat very quietly with her hand resting on Hamish's shoulder as he drove.

'I think I'm going to be a conductor when I grow up,' I announced, launching into an energetic impersonation in time to the classical music on the car radio.

'Who's going to cut my hair for me then?' Hamish demanded. 'I was counting on getting a special discount.'

I was taken aback. I hadn't expected him to remember about me wanting to be a hairdresser. Every time I spoke to Dad on the phone he asked me if I still wanted to be a detective even though I'd told him at least three times that I'd given up that idea now. I stared at the back of Hamish's head, feeling kind of strange.

The strange feeling was still with me after we got home and I was standing at the bathroom sink, brushing my teeth.

'I think I quite like Hamish,' I said, splattering toothpaste all over the bathroom mirror.

'Good.' Mum moved from the doorway to stand behind me, grabbing hold of my wrist. She's always fussy about the way I brush my teeth. 'How many times do I have to tell you, don't scrub so hard or you'll take off the enamel.' But she didn't sound cross. She sounded pleased.

'Mum . . .' Suddenly I really wanted to talk to her about how I felt about Dad and Hamish and everything.

'I'd better go back downstairs,' she sighed. 'I promised Hamish I'd make him some coffee.'

The warm feeling inside me vanished. 'Why can't he make his own coffee?' I snapped. It just popped out. I couldn't help it. I jerked my arm away from her.

'Laura . . .' She sounded exasperated.

I turned the cold tap on full blast, running my toothbrush under it. Water splashed everywhere. I felt furious and I didn't even know why. I mean, I liked Hamish now, didn't I?

She followed behind me as I stomped through to my bedroom. 'I thought you just said you liked—'

'So?' I jumped into bed and pulled the covers up over my head.

She waited for a few moments and I vowed that when she came over and sat on my bed and asked me what was wrong, I wasn't going to tell her. I didn't care if I hurt her feelings or not. She didn't care about my feelings so why should I care about hers?

She didn't come and sit on my bed. She gave the sort of sigh people give when they don't know what to do and are too tired to bother thinking about it any more. 'I'll see you in the morning, Laura.'

The minute she'd gone I jerked upright,

grabbed my pillow and hurled it as hard as I could at the door. She was a rotten traitor and I hated her. I wished I didn't have to see her in the morning. I wished I didn't have to see her ever again.

I glowered at my pillow lying humped over at the bottom of the door. The thought of having to get out of bed to pick it up made me madder still. 'I hate you!' I yelled as loudly as I could. Yelling it made me feel a bit better, but not much.

Chapter Eleven

I leaned deep into the freezer in Sainsbury's and lifted out the biggest packet of sausages I could find. The sausage sizzle was only four weeks away now. Janice was getting very jumpy because I hadn't even visited Guides with her yet. The other day she'd said she was getting to really like Helen. Last week Janice had been round to Helen's house for tea and this week Helen was coming back to Janice's. Mrs Bishop said she thought it was good for Janice and me to mix with other people and not just each other.

I'd told Janice that Mum was on the verge of changing her mind and letting me go to Guides. That wasn't exactly true – Mum was refusing even to discuss it – but I still hadn't given up hope completely.

Mum had been in a good mood for the whole of the past week. Not even the traffic jam out in the car park which had blocked our way to the bottle bank and nearly resulted in us slamming into the back of the brand-new BMW in front had ruffled her for more than a few minutes. Now she was gliding up and down the aisles with our trolley, lifting things from the shelves without consulting her list, nodding whenever I said, 'Can we have these?' and not even looking to see what the 'these' was.

'These sausages are the kind Janice is taking to the sausage sizzle,' I said, thrusting them hopefully into Mum's hand.

'Low fat. Very good. Much better for her arteries than the others.' She handed them back to me. 'I want you to stand in that queue and ask for four rashers of bacon – you know the kind Rory likes. I'm going to find the porridge oats. I'll be back in a minute.'

I scowled. Whenever Mum needs anything that involves queuing, she always sends me to do it. And she's never back in a minute. She's always back just as I'm getting served, by which time she's been round half the rest of the shop buying everything she wants and nothing that I want.

'Can't I go and get the porridge oats?'

'Darling, you're a much better queuer than I am. Hurry up, before it gets any bigger.'

I watched her disappear off in the direction of the cereals. Hamish was on night shift at Casualty this week, which meant he'd been finishing at eight o'clock in the morning and coming round to our house for his breakfast. Mum had started setting her alarm for seven instead of eight so that she was ready by the time he arrived. She'd been in such a good mood every morning that I'd begun to wish Hamish could be on night shift permanently, especially since it meant he had to be at work at eight o'clock in the evenings, after which I had Mum all to myself. She'd even started practising my Scottish dancing with me again before I went to bed, though she was so rusty she could hardly keep up with any of the steps.

I was doing a lot of practising at the moment, because my dance teacher wanted me to enter my first competition in two weeks' time. I needed to ask Mum to find my birth certificate because I had to have proof of my age. I also had to get her to buy me a kilt. So far I hadn't needed one, because at practice we just wore black leotards and tights. I wanted a new pair of black pumps too. The ones I had were all scuffed and smelly.

Mum's right about me getting less impatient standing in queues than she does. Whereas she's always sighing, fidgeting, checking her watch and muttering, 'This is ridiculous,' I tend to get completely distracted looking to see what other people have got in their trolleys. Everyone else's trolleys are always far more exciting than ours, chiefly because Mum is really mean about buying in anything that's bad for you. We're never allowed to have more than one packet of biscuits in the house at any one time and I bet you've never seen anyone push a trolley so fast past the confectionery shelves as she does. (Whenever I complain, Mum says I get more than my full entitlement of rubbish to eat at Janice's house as it is.)

Janice had told me yesterday that her mum was going to buy her a big packet of marshmallows so that we could wrap them in foil and roast them over the fire at the sausage sizzle. It sounded really good fun.

'Helen's not very pleased about you coming to Guides with us,' Janice had added. 'She thinks you'll take me away from her. She says I'm the only friend she's got at Guides.'

That figured. I couldn't imagine people waiting in queues to be friends with Helen.

'Yes, luv?'

I jumped. Like I said, it's amazing how quickly a queue can go down when you're busy daydreaming.

'Perfect timing!' Mum appeared at my side as the lady behind the counter was slicing Rory's bacon. 'Now all we need to do is find a checkout.'

Usually Mum gets just as impatient in the checkout queue as she does in any other queue and spends the whole time remembering different things she's forgotten and rushing off to fetch them. Today though, she stayed put.

'I've got something to ask you,' she said as I tried to balance on the base of the trolley without tipping it up. 'It's to do with Hamish.'

Something inside me went tight. I don't know what I expected her to say. That Hamish was moving in with us? That they were going to get married? I didn't feel ready for either of those things. Not yet.

'We want to go to Venice,' she said in a rush. 'It's meant to be really nice at this time of year so we thought we might go the week after next. What do you think?'

I frowned. 'Venice like in that film we saw the other night?' It had been a very slushy TV movie where the couple in it had kept snogging a lot in different gondolas.

Mum smiled. 'Venice like in Italy, Laura.' She said it as if she thought I didn't know Venice was a real place as well as being a place on the television.

I felt cross with her for making fun of me. 'I

don't want to go to Venice!' I snapped. 'I'll miss too much school.'

'Well, actually . . .' She flushed. 'You see, we sort of thought that while we were in Venice, you could stay with Marla. You could go to school from her house.'

I just stood there staring at her. I think I even forgot where I was for a moment or two. The supermarket and all the masses of people at the checkouts with all their masses of shopping seemed to exist at a huge distance away from me, as though nothing outside me was real at all. When Mum touched my arm, I jumped. That was real.

'It's just for a week, Laura. You don't mind too much, do you? You know what a good time you always have at Marla's.'

Something strange was happening inside me, as though everything soft was becoming hard. I stood absolutely still. Even my throat felt solid, like it had completely frozen up. I knew that if I opened my mouth nothing would come out and I wanted something to come out. I wanted something really savage and hurtful to come out, something that would make her feel as horrible as I felt right now.

'All right?' The checkout lady was waiting for us to put up our stuff. Mum began hurriedly to scoop things out of our trolley. I stood by stiffly, my arms folded. The minute the trolley was out of the way I slipped through to the other side of the till and ran out to the car park.

I was leaning against the bonnet of our car, trying to stop trembling, when Mum caught up with me.

'Laura, how DARE you run off like that!' She was furious. 'Open the boot!' She flung the car keys at me. They landed on the ground. I stared down at them. I felt weird. I felt as though Mum had changed, as if she had nothing to do with me at all.

'Pick up the keys,' she hissed.

And suddenly the numbness was gone and I was feeling angry, more angry than I'd felt in a long time. 'You love HIM more than you love me!' I bent down, lifted the keys and hurled them back at her. 'Go away with him!' I yelled. 'I don't care!'

She made to grab me, letting go of our trolley so that it ran into the side of the car next to ours. Swearing, she retrieved it, opened up the boot, and started to hurl our bags of shopping inside. Then she charged across the car park and crashed the empty trolley into the trolley bay.

I fled to the opposite side of the car as she returned. She looked fit to murder someone. I watched nervously as she unlocked the driver's door and got in.

I suddenly had a terrible panic that she was going to drive off and leave me there. 'Mum, I'm sorry,' I shouted at her through the glass.

She leaned across and unlocked the back passenger door. After I'd climbed in, she swivelled round to glare at me.

'So am I,' she replied tersely. 'Listen, Laura. I love you and Hamish in completely different ways. Do you understand that?'

I didn't understand. In fact, her saying that made me more furious than you can possibly imagine. I didn't care what way she loved him. I just cared that she didn't love him as much as she loved me. I mean, what if she *had* to choose between him and me? I pressed my lips together, tightly. It had happened to Dad, hadn't it? He'd had to choose. And he hadn't chosen me.

Chapter Twelve

I didn't remember about my birth certificate until the day before Mum and Hamish were due to go to Venice. We'd got the kilt sorted out. Mum had taken my waist measurement and the length measurement – I thought it was going to be too short, but Hamish insisted that kilts were meant to fall exactly to your knee and no more – and got Granny to send one down from Scotland. My Highland Dancing competition was the next weekend which meant Mum wasn't going to be there for it. She said she'd have made Venice a different weekend if she'd known and that it was my own fault for forgetting to tell her before they booked their flight. Mum had completely lost patience with all my complaining. They'd compromised by only going for a long weekend instead of the whole week and I should be satisfied with that, she said, and that it was high time I learned that the world didn't revolve around *me*.

That made me mad. I knew perfectly well that the world didn't revolve around me and if I needed any reminding then the photos of Dad with my new baby sister that my stepmother sent with her last email were quite sufficient. (I didn't tell you that my stepmother sometimes sends me emails, did I? Sometimes when I send one to Dad, I get a reply from her, using 'we' all the way through as if they've written it together, when in fact I can tell that it's just from her.)

Anyway, since complaining to Mum about Venice didn't work, I started trying to make Hamish feel guilty instead, but that didn't work either, because Hamish seemed to find my getting cross with him a source of great amusement. It wasn't horrible amusement. It was more like very fond amusement. All the same, it's irritating when you're trying hard to stay angry with a person and you end up laughing with them instead.

'I'll tell you what. If you're good, we'll bring you back some ice cream from Venice,' he'd tease, pulling a face at me, and I'd want to get cross, but the face he was pulling would be far too funny.

I didn't have any problems getting cross with Mum. I'd been feeling permanently angry with her recently, like I couldn't remember being since just after Dad left. I wasn't bothering to hide the fact either. The trouble was that even though I felt so angry with her I still didn't want her to go. Every time I thought of her leaving me to fly away with Hamish I felt like bursting into tears, but there was no way I was going to tell *her* that.

Last night when she'd come to kiss me good night, I'd immediately turned over in bed so as not to face her.

'Laura, I'll only be gone for three days.' The bed creaked as she sat down on it. Her body, touching my leg, felt warm. I moved my leg.

'Go for three *weeks* if you want,' I growled, then the thought of her actually leaving me for three whole weeks made me so furious, I added, 'Or three *years* even! I don't care!'

I'd lain awake for two hours after she'd gone, working myself up into a complete state. I didn't need Mum. I didn't need Dad. I didn't need anybody except myself. As soon as they left for Venice, I'd tell Marla I wasn't coming to stay with her after all, and I'd run away instead. I'd hitchhike up to Scotland or something and leave a note telling Mum I didn't want to see her ever again . . .

I started to cry at the thought of never seeing Mum ever again. It was all Hamish's fault. She'd never go away and leave me if it wasn't for him. I wished he'd fall into a canal in Venice and drown. I wished he'd get food poisoning from a bad ice cream and die.

I took a deep breath and turned over restlessly in bed. Why did Marla have to take their side too? 'Come on, Laura. Your mother hasn't had a proper holiday since your father left.' And why had I had to snap, 'So by "proper" you mean without me?' and ended up having a huge row with Mum and getting sent to my room? I felt as though nobody was on my side, not even Janice, who was so excited about the sausage sizzle she hardly even listened if you tried to talk about anything else.

I didn't bother asking Mum if I could go through her things to look for my birth certificate. I knew she'd be mad if she caught me doing it but I didn't care. I almost wanted her to catch me doing it. I felt like having a fight with her, which was why I wasn't being particularly quiet as I rummaged through the desk in her bedroom, messing up all the little compartments and not bothering to shut the little drawer in the top properly after I'd raked through that.

I started to search through the main drawers. The top one was stuffed full of old payslips and bank statements and boring stuff like that. The second drawer was jammed and I had a job to slide it open. The thing that was jamming it was a white plastic bag full of papers or something. I took it out and opened it. It was full of notebooks. They looked quite old. I opened one of them. It was a diary. Mum's name was written in faded ink on the first page. The date was written there too. I did a quick calculation in my head. Mum must have been ten when she wrote this. I started to feel a bit dizzy. I hadn't realized Mum had kept her old diaries. I flicked over to where the writing started in this one. It was messy but you could still read it. It turned out to be a pretty boring entry, all about which relatives had come to dinner (it being New Year's Day) and what food they had had to eat. There was no mention of Kathleen.

I emptied the bag on to the floor. I could hardly make myself sit still as I arranged all the diaries in chronological order. I took a deep breath as I found the one I wanted, the diary for the year Kathleen had died.

I went out on to the landing to listen. I could hear Mum and Hamish laughing in the kitchen. Quickly, I slipped back into Mum's room and closed the door. My heart was beating very fast as I carefully opened the diary at the first page:

'JANUARY 1ST – We weren't allowed to stay up

to see the New Year in last night. Mum says we'll be old enough next year, Kathleen as well, which I don't think is fair. How can we both be old enough at the same time? Kathleen was going on and on today about how I've eaten all the sweets I got for Christmas. She's still got half of hers left. I told Kathleen if she didn't shut up I'd eat the head off her chocolate Santa and she started crying and went running off to Mum like she always does, so I got into trouble. I HATE HER! I wish I didn't have a sister. I wish—'

'LAURA!' Mum was yelling to me up the stairs.

Panicking, I stuffed all the other diaries back into their bag and shoved it back in the drawer. I slipped the one I was reading into my pocket just as Mum pushed open the door.

'What are you doing in here?'

'Nothing.'

'What are you doing in my desk?'

I scrambled to my feet. I'd left the top of the desk open. 'Looking for my birth certificate,' I mumbled, avoiding her gaze. 'I need it for dancing. The competition needs proof of our age.'

She looked irritated. 'How utterly ridiculous. I'm hardly going to lie about your age just to have you win a medal in some Highland Dancing competition.'

'You might.' I stuck out my bottom lip. 'If you really wanted me to win.'

She looked even more irritated. 'You shouldn't be going through my desk like that anyway. If you want something of mine then you ask me first.'

'It's not something of yours. It's *my* birth certificate, isn't it?'

'Laura, I'm warning you . . .' I knew that the only thing stopping her from blowing up at me was that she didn't want to fall out with me just before going off to Venice.

'Ladies, are you coming?' Hamish called up the stairs.

Mum frowned. 'I came upstairs to ask if you want to go to the park.' She held up her hand to cancel out my answer before I'd even had a chance to give it. 'Forget that. I'm not asking. I'm telling. Go and get your coat. Hurry up.' She stood holding the door open for me.

In my room, I hid the diary under my mattress. I knew it wasn't a very original place, but I'd think of somewhere better when I had more time. I really wished I could sit down and read through it straightaway. I wished I knew the exact date

Kathleen had died. At least then I'd be able to turn to the right page immediately without having to read through the whole thing.

'LAURA!'

'Coming!' I grabbed my coat and raced downstairs to join them.

The funny thing about that afternoon in the park was that, even though I was dying to get back to Mum's diary, I quite enjoyed it. We'd taken some bread to feed the ducks, and Hamish and I ended up having a competition to see who could hit the most ducks on the head. (When Mum accused us of being childish I protested that I *was* a child and Hamish said he *felt* like a child and did that count?) After we'd walked right round the park we bought ice creams from the shop and when I pointed out to Mum that ice creams had hundreds and hundreds of calories, she just laughed and said that today she didn't care. That afternoon I almost felt that if Mum and Hamish did stay together, it mightn't be such a bad thing after all.

When we got back to the house it was teatime. 'It's such a nice day, we could eat outside,' Hamish suggested. 'What about a barbecue?'

Mum and I looked at each other. I could tell she knew that the mention of a barbecue had reminded me about the sausage sizzle. 'We could have one if you like,' she answered calmly. 'Though someone will have to go out and buy something to cook on it.'

'Mrs Bishop has got tonnes of sausages in her freezer for Janice to take to the sausage sizzle,' I said pointedly to Mum. 'She's got marshmallows too.' I took a deep breath. 'Mum, please can I join the Guides? I really want to go to the sausage sizzle with Janice. I know you're worried because of what happened to Kathleen but I'll be really careful—'

'LAURA!' Her eyes were nearly bulging out of their sockets. 'I don't want you talking about Kathleen any more! I've had enough! Do you understand?'

I didn't bother to answer. What was the point?

'It's OK. I don't want a stupid barbecue anyway,' I snapped. I turned my back on her and left the room.

Upstairs, I shut my bedroom door and pushed a chair up against it. Then I fished Mum's diary out from under my mattress. Flicking through it quickly, I discovered that the second half of the book was empty. She must have got fed up and stopped writing it. The last entry on the twenty-third of June was scrawled in huge untidy letters:

'I HATE HER! She ALWAYS gets Mum on her side. Just because HER hair looks all pretty with a ribbon in it Mum says I'VE got to wear one to Guides tomorrow as well. My hair looks stupid with a ribbon. Everyone's going to laugh. I want to take it out before we get there, but I know that if I do she'll tell on me when we get home. It's not fair! I used to love Guides before SHE joined. Now all she does is spy on me and report back to Mum all the time. Anyway, I've figured out a way to get rid of her once and for all! I'm going to try it out tomorrow! I'll let you know if it works!'

And that was it. There was nothing else written in the book. It was really frustrating. I flicked through the blank pages again, just to check, and then I saw it. At the top of one page, about a week later, a single small tidy sentence was printed: 'Kathleen's funeral was today.'

I dropped the diary. I felt sick.

Chapter Thirteen

I didn't say anything to Mum that evening. Call me
a coward if you like, but would you be able to
march downstairs and ask *your* mother if she'd
murdered her little sister twenty-three years ago?
Wouldn't you rather just convince yourself that
there had to be some other explanation because,
let's face it, your mum was your mum and there
was no possible way she could ever have murdered
anybody? I mean, the whole idea was completely
fantastical. I refused to even think about it any
more.

The trouble was that, even though I refused to
think about it, I still felt terrible. I just said I
wasn't hungry when Mum wanted to know why I
couldn't eat up all my tea, and when I woke up
sweating in the night with a really scary dream, I
didn't do what I usually do when I have bad night-
mares, which is to go into Mum's room. Instead, I
did what Mrs Bishop (who never lets her children
wake her up in the middle of the night) says you
should do if you have a bad dream. I turned on to

my other side and tried to imagine some sheep in my head so I could count them.

I was really groggy when Mum got me up the next morning – the sheep had taken ages to work – and I was glad I'd got all my things ready the night before to take to Marla's.

'Here.' Mum handed me my kilt as I rolled out of bed. 'Try this on again. I've altered the button.'

I took it from her and wrapped it round my waist, fastening it over the top of my pyjama bottoms. The thought of my Highland Dancing competition this afternoon made me feel ill. I stood stiffly as Mum hugged me and kissed my hair and said, 'I wish I was coming to see you dance today. I will be there next time, I promise.'

'Unless you're on call or something.' I pulled away from her, undoing the kilt. 'What time is Marla coming?' She was feeling bad about leaving me behind, I knew, but I didn't feel like helping her to feel any better.

When she'd gone downstairs to join Hamish – he'd stayed the night last night – I put on my jeans and my favourite top, which she'd ironed for me yesterday. Like I said before, it's usually unheard of for Mum to iron anything a whole twenty-four hours in advance, and her having done it now made me feel even worse. It reminded me of the last time Mum had lain out all my clothes in readiness for me like this, which was on the morning of Grandpa's funeral in Scotland. That morning Mum had been really tense too and there had been the same we're-all-going-to-burst-into-tears-if-we're-not-careful sort of atmosphere. I remember Mum had nearly had a fit because Dad said he thought I was too young to go to the funeral.

'There's no such thing as being too young to go to a funeral! Children need to say goodbye the same as everybody else!'

'Well, let's hear what Laura thinks shall we?'

'Don't you *dare* do that to her! Don't you dare make her take sides!'

'Why? Because you're afraid she'll take *my* side?'

I suddenly realized I was breathing very fast indeed. I had that horrible, gnawing, wanting-something feeling again right in my middle. I sat down on my bed, hugging myself, taking quick, sharp breaths, trying to slow them down to longer, slower breaths, counting each one from one to ten over and over, like Mum had shown me when I'd had these panicky feelings before. I used to get them quite often for a long time after Dad left, at least Mum said it was to do with Dad leaving. I thought it was really unfair, the way she blamed everything on that. I mean, I know I stopped doing so well at school after he left but it wasn't because I was sitting there missing him or anything. I don't really know why it was, except that I just couldn't be bothered to race Janice any more to see who could get their sums done quickest, or put up my hand when I knew the answer to one of our teacher's questions. I hardly ever did my home-work either, and Mum seemed to have forgotten there was any such thing as homework until she got called up to the school about it. She got much stricter with me after that, but in the end what made me start working properly again was the way she kept blaming every spelling mistake I made or sum I got wrong on the adverse effect of Dad's leaving until I just couldn't stand it any longer.

Downstairs I could hear the front door being opened and Mum and Marla's voices, high-pitched, in the hall. I glanced at the time on my alarm clock. We would have to leave for the airport soon. We were all going in Marla's car, then Marla and I were going back to her house.

'Laura, I know you don't want us to miss our plane, so could you get a move on, please?' Mum shouted up the stairs.

I glanced round my room to see if I'd forgotten anything, then I slipped my hand under the mattress and pulled out Mum's diary. I put it on top of the other stuff in my bag and zipped it up.

I went downstairs. They were all in the kitchen. Mum was standing at the sink, vigorously splashing soapy water over the breakfast dishes. She wasn't wearing her rubber gloves, which she usually only neglects to do if she's in a very bad mood or a very major flap about something. Hamish and Marla were sitting at the kitchen table watching her warily. Mum turned when I came into the room, and said carefully, 'Laura, I made you cup of tea but it's gone cold. Do you want some cereal or something?'

'Hadn't we better get moving, Sylvie?' Hamish said, tapping his watch before I could reply. 'We don't know what the traffic to the airport's going to be like.' He grinned good-naturedly at me as he added, 'Now, Laura, as Italy is the home of the *ice-a-cream-a* please tell us *what-a* flavour you would like us to bring home for you!'

I would have laughed at his pathetic attempt to talk in a funny Italian accent (which I know was meant to cheer me up) but Mum suddenly snapped, 'For God's sake, Hamish, stop teasing her, will you?' and glared at him as if she couldn't stand the sight of him any longer.

Hamish looked taken aback.

I stared at her in astonishment.

Before anyone had a chance to say anything else, Marla stood up quickly, placed her hands on my shoulders and firmly propelled me out of the door. 'Let's fetch your things from upstairs, shall we?'

I only made a pretence of joining in as Marla noisily flapped round my room checking for things I might have forgotten to pack. I was too busy straining to hear what was happening downstairs. Were they having a row? Was Mum going to change her mind about going to Venice with him? Presently I heard the phone tinkle in Mum's room, which meant the phone downstairs was being put down. Who had they been phoning? What was going on?

Marla was unzipping my bag to put my slippers inside. 'What are you doing with this?' She was taking Mum's diary out of the bag. I froze. I knew from the way she was holding it that she recognized what it was.

She looked right into my eyes. 'What are you doing with this?' she repeated.

I opened my mouth but no words came out.

'Laura . . .'

'I'm just borrowing it,' I mumbled.

'And your mother knows?'

I stared at her, terrified. Lying to Marla was a pretty suicidal thing to do. Oliver used to lie to her all the time and as far as I remember, even with all that experience, he never managed to get away with it. But if I told her the truth –

'Laura, does your mother know you've got this?' She looked so stern my knees started to tremble.

I didn't answer. I was starting to back towards the door.

'Got what?' Mum demanded. I jumped. I'd backed straight into her. How long had she been there? How much had she heard? Had she seen the diary? How could I possibly escape before Marla had a chance to tell on me?

'Listen, we've just booked a taxi to take us to the airport. We think it'll be easier.' She was frowning at my terrified expression. 'Laura, I'll only be gone for three days.' And suddenly, to my absolute horror, she started to cry.

Marla instantly stepped forward, holding the diary out of sight, saying firmly, 'Don't be ridiculous, Sylvie. Laura's a big girl. Of course she can

124

cope with you going away for such a short while. Can't you, Laura?'

And suddenly, because Mum was crying, I really wanted her to have her holiday with Hamish, even though I still didn't want her to leave me. It was all really confusing. 'It's OK, Mum,' I said, rushing to fetch my box of multicoloured tissues to offer her one.

Mum gave a weak smile, sniffing as she pulled out a tissue. Marla zipped up my bag again and handed it to me to carry. I didn't know where she'd put the diary but I didn't care, just so long as she didn't let Mum see it.

Hamish was standing in the hall, clutching Rory. 'He promises to be good,' he announced, raising Rory's right paw and pulling a solemn Boy Scout face on his behalf.

'Marla, are you sure this is OK?' Mum flapped.

'Sylvie, stop panicking. Laura is in charge of the cat and I am in charge of her. What could possibly go wrong?'

I stood with Mum, holding Rory, while Hamish and Marla carried the things out to the taxi, which had just arrived.

'Remember what happened with Dad's taxi when he was on his way to the airport?' I murmured, rubbing my face against Rory's head. When Dad had called in to say goodbye to me, he'd kept his taxi waiting so long that it had nearly driven off without him. (Secretly I'd been praying that it *would* drive off without him and that he'd miss his plane and have to come back and stay with us and that while he was staying with us he'd decide that he didn't really want to leave after all.)

'Laura . . .' Mum looked close to tears again and I suddenly had a horrible feeling that I'd mentioned Dad deliberately to make her feel bad. But I didn't really want her to feel bad.

I dropped Rory and flung my arms around her, clinging to her really tightly. I didn't even care that Rory had shot out the front door and that Marla was shouting to Hamish to catch him and nearly having a fit.

The taxi tooted again. It reminded me of Dad's taxi, tooting its horn over and over. Tears were starting at the backs of my eyes. I felt completely helpless and horrible, like I wasn't going to see Mum again for a very long time, even though I knew I was going to see her again in three days.

As their taxi disappeared from view I felt incredibly empty. I felt as though a giant hand had reached right down into me and scooped out all my insides. Then I felt as though Hamish and Mum had taken my insides with them. Marla put her arm round me. 'Come on. Now that your mother's out of the way, let's go and find the chocolate biscuits.'

While Marla was making tea in the kitchen, I sat in the front room cuddling Rory, who we'd managed to entice back into the house with us.

I thought Rory looked sad, as if he was missing Mum already too. 'She'll be back in three days,' I told him sternly. 'Three days is hardly any time at all.'

I was trying to work out how long three days actually was in cat-time (because our vet told us that one year for a cat is the same as five years for a human being) when Marla swept into the room carrying a tray.

'Tea,' she announced. Sitting on the tray, between the teapot and the chocolate digestives, was Mum's diary.

I stared at the grubby little book. I couldn't believe I'd completely forgotten about it like that.

'I think we should have a little talk about this now, don't you?' Marla said, putting down the tray very carefully and picking up the diary.

Chapter Fourteen

As soon as I'd finished telling everything to Marla I felt like I'd betrayed Mum and I started sobbing all over again. Mum would never come back from Venice now. Not when she found out I'd read her diary. Not when she knew that I knew about Kathleen –

'Laura, stop that crying. It's giving me a headache.' Marla was frowning. 'I don't know what to say. I know your mother wanted to wait until you were older before she told you about Kathleen. She thought you'd understand it better then.'

'Understand *what*?'

'Well, understand that . . . Understand that what happened was . . .' She sort of gasped and stood up. 'No. It's not right for me to tell you this.'

'But—'

'Come on.'

'But—' I wanted to know. I had to know. I wasn't going anywhere until she told me.

'Hurry up.' She flung my coat at me. 'We're

going to the airport. If we're fast we might still catch them.'

Of course, there turned out to be sixty million sets of red traffic lights between our house and Birmingham Airport, and then Marla was in such a rush she missed one of the turn-offs and we lost about ten minutes trying to get back en route again.

'Why am I doing this? I must be crazy!' she kept wailing at two-minute intervals, while I sat holding in my breath, praying over and over again for the plane to be delayed and for them to still be at the airport.

'Laura, we're not going to make it. I'm sorry,' Marla said as we turned into the road leading to the airport building. 'Not unless their flight's been delayed, and even then they've probably already gone through to sit in the departure lounge.'

'*You'll* have to tell me about Kathleen then,' I answered fiercely.

She sighed. 'Just go inside and have a look round for them while I park the car.' She drew up at the taxi rank to let me out.

It wasn't very crowded inside the airport building. Straight ahead of me were loads of check-in desks with several queues of people lined up with their baggage.

I stood still and scanned the place, searching for them. I could hear my heart thumping really loudly in my chest. Please be here. Please be here. A middle-aged lady stopped dragging her suitcase to ask if I was all right.

'Yes,' I nodded. 'Yes. I'm looking for my mum.'

'Are you lost?' Her face creased up in concern.

'No. No!' I ran off in the direction of the check-in desks before she could interfere any more. Grown-ups are terrible when they start thinking you're lost. They don't listen to a word you say because they're so busy panicking at the thought of having to do something about you.

I suddenly saw the check-in desk for Venice straight ahead of me. There was one couple standing there putting their bags on to the little conveyor belt. I walked up to stand behind them. Where was Mum? If she was in the departure lounge already, would they let me through to speak to her? Was there time for her to come back through to speak to me?

'Laura! Thank God!' Marla was looking flushed and hassled, hurrying towards me with her car keys in one hand and her handbag in the other.

'I've parked on double yellow lines. I'm bound to get a ticket. I might even get the car towed away. I'd better go back and move it! Have you found out if they've gone through? I expect they have. This is all my fault, getting you wound up like this. I wasn't thinking. I'm really sorry, darling.' She seemed completely harassed and exhausted.

'Marla. Look!' I could hardly believe my eyes but there was Mum, closely followed by Hamish, heading towards the check-in desk where we were standing.

'Mum!' I called, jumping up and down and waving madly.

'Laura!' Mum came rushing up to me and put down her bags.

'What's going on?' Hamish asked as he joined us. Now the four of us were standing in a little huddle, causing an obstruction at the check-in desk.

'Thank goodness we caught you,' Marla said.

'You nearly didn't,' Mum said. 'I was having second thoughts about going, so Hamish took me for a cup of tea to calm me down. But why are you here? Has something happened?'

'It's nothing to worry about,' Marla said quickly. 'It's just that Laura's got something she badly

131

needs to ask you. Laura, why don't you and your mum go and sit down over there for a minute?' She pointed to a row of empty seats nearby, while at the same time pulling Mum's diary out of her bag and handing it to her. 'Here. Laura's read the last page of this and she's rather distressed by it. She thinks she knows what happened to Kathleen.' She exchanged a long, hard look with my mother. 'It wasn't my place to tell her, Sylvie, and she needs to be told. It's not fair to make her wait until you come back.' She turned to me again. 'Laura, take your mother over there and tell her what you told me. Go on. It'll be all right.'

I gave Marla a helpless look. I wasn't so sure.

'Mum, I didn't mean to read it,' I panicked, the minute we were sitting down with no one around to overhear us. 'I found it by accident . . .' I was leaning further and further away from her. I was close to tears. It suddenly seemed to me that Mum was a complete stranger, not my mother at all, as she sat quite still reading the diary laid open on her lap.

Her face was flushed and tense-looking. 'What did you think when you read this, Laura?'

'It's just that . . . I know you hated her and you

wanted to get rid of her and . . . But I know you couldn't have . . . It's just that . . .' I started to sob, feeling worse than I'd ever felt in my whole life, worse even than on the day Dad left. 'I don't know. I don't know. I don't know.' I had moved a whole seat away from her now. I wanted to run away, to take back everything I'd said, to put back the diary and pretend I'd never found it, to never ask any questions about Kathleen ever again. I was too frightened to find out the truth. I was too frightened in case it meant losing Mum.

I had to wait a long time before she started to speak and all that time my heart was pounding as I watched her face. She moved to sit on the empty seat between us so that she was sitting right beside me again. 'Laura, I'm so sorry.' She put her arm round me, holding me so tightly that I couldn't escape, couldn't separate from her. 'It's true, I was very jealous of Kathleen when I was a little girl. I always felt she was my parents' favourite and when she came to Guides and she was put in my patrol . . .' She grimaced. 'I felt as though she'd stolen the one thing I had that was all *mine*, especially when my mother stopped asking *me* about what we did at Guides and started asking Kathleen instead.'

133

She paused, staring down at the diary. 'I wanted her to stop coming to Guides – that's what I meant by "get rid" of her – because having her there spoilt it for me.' Mum paused again. She had been speaking calmly, but now her eyes were glistening like she was holding back tears.

'So what happened?' I whispered.

'It was an accident, Laura. We were about to line up for inspection that day and I was feeling jealous of how pretty Kathleen looked, so I pulled her ribbon out of her hair and a few of us started tossing it about between us while she tried to get it back.' Mum swallowed. 'And of course she started crying and saying that she'd tell our mum, so I told her not to be such a crybaby, and some of my friends joined in. They started chanting, "Crybaby, crybaby," and she ran out of the hall. I felt guilty then and I ran out after her, but when I got outside I heard this terrible screeching of brakes and someone was sounding their horn and Kathleen was running across the road and a car was coming and . . .' Mum's voice went hoarse.

I stared at her, completely stunned. Inside my head I was hearing Mum calling Kathleen a crybaby and I was seeing Kathleen, who looked so sweet and pretty in all her photos, being hit by a car and never coming back to life again. I felt a bit sick.

'It was an accident but it was my fault,' Mum finished shakily. 'That's why I couldn't bear to see you in a Girl Guide uniform. That's why I was so angry when you ran out in front of Mr Bishop's car that day. It brought it all back, you see . . .'

And I did see. I saw that Mum wasn't a murderer – of course she wasn't! But she still felt responsible for her sister's death. And that was why she had been acting so strangely.

'Sylvie, the flight's boarding.' Suddenly Marla was standing beside us, looking anxious. 'Are you two all right?'

I wasn't all right, and I didn't think Mum was either.

When neither of us spoke, Marla said urgently, 'You'll have to go now if you're going to make the flight, Sylvie.'

'You know what?' Mum said in a trembly voice. 'I really don't think I *should* go away this weekend. Not after what I've just told Laura. I can't just leave her after burdening her with all this.'

'You haven't burdened me,' I murmured. I wasn't sure how to explain it to her, but if anything she had taken a burden *away*. Suddenly I thought of something. 'Remember how you used to say that children should always be told the truth because otherwise they'll imagine something far worse?' I reminded her.

Mum looked at me as if she was dimly remembering a time when she used to make such confident statements. 'Did I say that?'

I nodded.

'Sylvie,' Marla said firmly, 'I think you really need this holiday. Don't you agree, Laura?' She looked at me then, with an expression that was urging me to say the right thing.

I was tempted to say that *I* needed Mum at home with *me* this weekend but when I saw how utterly exhausted Mum looked my insides gave a sort of pang. I didn't want her to be like that. Maybe if she went away this weekend with Hamish, then he could help her feel better again.

Slowly I nodded. 'Yes.' I still had a lot more questions I wanted to ask about Kathleen, but I knew they could wait.

Simultaneously Mum and I looked across to where Hamish was waiting patiently at the check-in desk. I don't know what was going through her mind right then, but *I* couldn't help thinking that if Dad were here, he'd be shouting his head off at Mum right now, for taking so long.

'I'll be fine,' I said, feeling more grown up than I'd ever felt in my life before. 'Go on, Mum. It's OK.'

After they'd gone, Marla took me to buy some chocolate from the airport shop (because she says that chocolate nearly always makes you feel better in times of stress).

'Are you all right now, Laura?' she asked as we headed outside together, munching our chocolate raisins.

I nodded, yawning. I suddenly felt really tired, as if all I wanted was a very long sleep.

'Aargh!' Marla burst out as we approached her car.

I stared at it in awe. 'I've never been with anyone who's had their car wheel-clamped before!' I exclaimed excitedly.

And all I can say about the look Marla gave me then, is that if looks could kill, I certainly wouldn't be sitting here now, telling you this story.

Chapter Fifteen

I didn't do very well in the Highland Dancing competition, though Marla and my dance teacher said I deserved a medal just for keeping going in the Sword Dance after I accidentally hit one of the swords with my toe and sent it skating right across the stage.

Mum and Hamish didn't fall out of any gondolas in Venice, but arrived home safe and sound just as they'd promised. Of course I asked Hamish straight away where my ice cream was, and he promptly produced a strawberry Cornetto (my favourite kind), which he tried to say had come all the way from Italy even though I knew it had come straight from the freezer at the corner shop.

Mum told me she'd done a lot of thinking while she was away and she'd decided I could join the Guides after all, and go to the sausage sizzle. I couldn't believe it. I ran straight across to Janice's house to tell her. Of course Janice wanted to know all about Mum and Kathleen and everything. That was difficult, because I felt like I ought to tell her a bit of the truth, which is quite a tricky thing to do really, much trickier than just lying. In the end, I told her that Kathleen had been knocked down by a car while she was on her way home from Guides and that was why Mum got so upset at the thought of me in a Guide uniform.

'How come she doesn't mind any more then?' Janice demanded after I'd actually started going to Guides with her.

I looked away. 'I'm not sure,' I mumbled.

I wasn't going to explain to Janice about the difference Mum says talking it over with Hamish, and with the counsellor she's started seeing up at the hospital, has made to the way she feels. The fact is, Mum can now look at me in my Guide uniform without wincing – which is more than I can say for myself!

The other thing that's happened recently is that Dad phoned to invite me to go and stay with him for four whole weeks this summer. Mum and Hamish are coming to Australia too – though they're going to travel round on their own while I stay with Dad. I can't wait! I'll be meeting my new baby sister for the first time then too. I'm quite nervous about that, as well as excited. Mum says I've not to worry if I *feel* a bit jealous of the baby, because jealousy is a natural feeling. She says I can phone her on her mobile any time I want to talk about it.

Maybe I'll feel jealous of Daisy (that's my little sister's name, by the way), or maybe I won't – I guess that will depend a lot on Dad. But in any case, I'm going to try my hardest to be nice to her.

The sausage sizzle was really good fun just as Janice had predicted, even though my sausages kept falling into the fire when I wasn't looking, and getting burnt. (I think Helen had something to do with that, but I couldn't prove it.)

After that though, I sort of went off the idea of being a Guide. 'It's not that I hate all of it,' I tried to explain diplomatically to Janice (because I still wanted her to be my best friend and not Helen's). 'It's just that I don't *feel* like a Guide, that's all. I don't *want* to wear the same boring uniform as everybody else. And I hate being bossed about by that stupid patrol leader. It's worse than school.'

As I tried to explain to Mum – even more diplomatically since she'd just spent loads of money on my Guide uniform – I felt much more *me*, doing my Highland Dancing. 'So, is it OK if I don't go to Guides any more?' I begged.

She stopped struggling to open Rory's cat-food

and pointed the tin-opener at me accusingly. 'You, young lady, are really pushing your luck.'

'But it's dead boring. And it's all girls. I don't think it's good for me to go to something that's all girls. I mean, some of the girls at school have got boyfriends already and they didn't meet them by going to Guides.'

Mum's eyes widened considerably. 'I beg your pardon?'

'What are we fighting about now, ladies?' Hamish came into the kitchen carrying an empty coffee mug and the newspaper. He dropped the mug in the sink and took the tin opener out of Mum's hand. 'Here. Let me. It's impossible to have a really good argument while trying to feed a cat.'

I giggled and Mum's face relaxed. All the same, I could almost feel the next battle just around the corner. I won't ask you to stick around for that, because I'm sure you've got plenty of battles of your own to be getting on with. I'm quite glad Hamish is here though. Having him around helps a lot. I've got this funny feeling that for the next few years, as far as battles with Mum are concerned, I'm going to need all the help I can get. But so is Mum!

The Mum Hunt

Another exciting story from

Gwyneth Rees

❀ 1 ❀

It all started in French. Well, sort of. I was sitting in French, which was our last lesson that day, feeling fidgety because I'd already finished my work and I had nothing left to do. I was dying to speak to Holly. Holly is my best friend and I'd been waiting all day to ask her advice about something. Holly is an expert at knowing what to do in difficult situations. She says it's because her mum treats her like a grown-up and lets her watch anything she wants on TV and ask any questions she wants about it afterwards. Sometimes Holly and her mum stay up late discussing all sorts of things, which makes me really envious because I'm not allowed to stay up late to discuss anything at all.

Anyway, Holly had been away at the dentist all morning, otherwise I'd have spoken to her earlier. If we'd had an afternoon break I'd have spoken to her then, but our school has abolished

1

afternoon breaks so we can finish earlier like they do on the Continent or something. That means we're expected to go from lunchtime until three o'clock without talking to each other, which if you ask me is a form of *child abuse*. Well, it is for me. I'm a bit of a chatterbox, at least, that's what Dad says. Matthew, my brother, calls me a stuck record which I object to because it implies that I say the same things over and over again, which I don't. He says our great-aunt Esmerelda could talk the hind leg off a donkey too, and that's why I got named after her, but Dad says I got named after her because my mother really liked the name. Nobody calls me, Esmerelda, though. They all call me Esmie for short.

Anyway, that afternoon we'd been set an exercise by our French teacher, Miss Murphy (who'd left the room to sort out the teacherless class next door) that involved translating a whole list of different types of food from English into French.

'Guess what?' I hissed, leaning over to see how my friend was getting on with her answers.

'Get off!' Holly pushed my hand away as I tried to pencil in the word *pomme* for her next to apple. 'I *can* do this myself, you know, Esmie!'

'Sorry.' It's just that Juliette, our au pair, is

2

French, and I've started getting top marks in French at school ever since she came. Holly swears she's not jealous but she gets pretty annoyed with me for always finishing things before she does.

'Last night Juliette came up with this idea – and I want to know what *you* think of it!' I announced.

Holly looked at me. I knew that would get her attention.

But I wanted to tell her the whole story – from the beginning – so I did.

'It started when Juliette said something in French that Matthew didn't understand but I did!' I began, proudly. (Dad has this idea that he can use Juliette to turn Matthew and me into fluent French speakers overnight if he gets her to talk to us in nothing but French. Unfortunately Juliette came to England to practise her English, so there's been a bit of a clash.)

Holly crinkled up her nose. 'I think it's really daft, your dad making you talk French every meal time.'

'It's not *every* meal time. We're allowed to speak English at breakfast and lunch and all day if we want at the weekends. Anyway, Matthew didn't understand her and I did!'

'So?' Holly grunted, going back to her work.

Holly doesn't understand what it's like to have to compete all the time with an older brother for your parent's attention. She's eleven like me, but she's an only child. Her parents are divorced and they compete with each other all the time for *her* attention. They had a big fight about who would get custody of her and now it's shared, so Holly spends one night a week and every second weekend with her dad and the rest of the time with her mum. She's got two of everything: two bedrooms, two wardrobes and two toothbrushes. The only thing she hasn't got two of yet is mothers and fathers. Neither of her parents have found anyone else, though Holly reckons it won't be long before one of them does and she's dreading that.

I continued to talk despite the fact that she looked like she wasn't listening. 'We were sitting eating our dinner when Juliette started telling Dad – in French – all about this advert she'd seen in the lonely-hearts column which she said would be perfect for him! Dad nearly choked on his *pommes de terre*.' I pointed to the empty space on Holly's page next to potatoes and waited for her to fill it in.

'What did your dad say?' Holly put down her pencil, looking interested now.

'Something in French I didn't understand

but I think it was pretty rude. Then the telephone rang and it was Dad's work and they'd just found a dead body or something and that ruined everything as usual. But then, after he'd gone out, Juliette showed us the advert and—'

'A *dead body*?' Holly always gets excited by any gruesome details I let out about Dad's work. Dad is a police detective which Holly reckons is really cool. 'Was it murdered?'

'How should I know?' I wasn't meant to know about it at all and Dad would kill me if he knew I was talking about it to Holly. 'Look, never mind that! I want to know what you think about *this*.' I rummaged around in my schoolbag and pulled out a crumpled piece of newspaper, but before I could show it to her our French teacher strode back into the room and stopped at the first desk she came to.

Which happened to be ours . . .

'What's this?' Before I knew what was happening she had grabbed the lonely-hearts column from my hand.

I was horrified. Miss Murphy is fortyish, with round spectacles and very flat hair and she looks like she wouldn't know what to do with a lonely heart if it jumped out and hit her in the face. And she couldn't possible miss *this* lonely heart because it was ringed with Juliette's red pen.

'It's her dad's, Miss,' Holly said, quickly, pointing at me.

I scowled at her. The rest of the class had stopped talking and the silence was horrible. I could feel them all staring.

'Is that right, now?' Miss Murphy has a really strong Irish accent and she wears a big silver cross round her neck which Holly says means she's a Catholic. I don't know much about religion seeing as how Dad never takes us to church. Holly doesn't go to church either, but, like I said before, her mum tells her things – too much, my dad says.

Miss Murphy began to read the advertisement out loud, slowly, like she was just a beginner-reader. *'Beautiful, blue-eyed, blonde botanist WLTM . . .'* she recited, raising her voice so she could still be heard above the sniggers coming from everybody else. 'W . . . L . . . T . . . M . . .' she repeated, carefully. She looked at both of us for help.

Holly nudged me. 'Esmie.' Like I was the expert.

'Would Like To Meet,' I croaked, feeling so embarrassed I wanted to die.

'Would like to meet a *handsome, plant-loving,*

man in uniform!' Miss Murphy let out a noise like a muffled snort, which is a habit of hers. Our class were all laughing really loudly now. 'Do you think these criteria would be fitting your daddy, then, Esmie?'

I was bright red and trembling by this time. I could have killed Holly. Why couldn't she just have said we'd *found* the paper or something?

I shook my head, helplessly. I was so embarrassed I couldn't even speak.

'He's no good with plants, Miss,' Holly said.

The whole class laughed even louder.

'But he *is* a policeman!' Holly added, starting to sound like she was enjoying herself.

'Is that so?' Miss Murphy's eyes were sparkling wickedly. 'Well, it sounds like this . . .' She glanced again at the advert. '. . . this *lady botanist* prefers men in uniform, so maybe he's still in with a chance!'

'Only he's plain clothed, Miss,' Holly put in, frowning. 'Isn't he, Esmie? He's a detective, Miss, so he has to be plain clothed so his murderers don't recognize him.'

I found my voice then. 'That's not true!' I spluttered. 'He has to show his murderers his badge before he asks them anything!' Goodness knows why I said that.

Miss Murphy's face went pink and she

started to chortle. It wasn't a pretty sight. 'Well, perhaps if he's got a badge, that will make up for him not having a uniform,' she teased.

'Only if it's a really *sexy* badge!' one of the boys called out.

I wanted to crawl under my desk and never come out again. Or at the very least, move out of the area and change my name so no one would ever be able to trace me.

As the bell rang, Miss Murphy shouted at the class that for our homework she wanted us to write out pretend advertisements to go in a French lonely-hearts column. Then she started laughing again. She gave the advertisement back to me and rushed out of the classroom, no doubt in order to tell everyone in the staffroom.

'Holly, *why* did you have to do that?' I snapped, as I stuffed the piece of newspaper as far down into the bottom of my bag as it would go.

'Don't blame me!' she said, looking offended. 'He's *your* father!'

'Hey, Esmie?' one of the boys called out to me.

I looked up. It was Billy Sanderson, who usually only speaks to me when he wants to copy my homework and then acts all spiteful for the rest of the week because I won't let him. He was standing in the doorway with all his mates.

'Miss Murphy's single! What do you reckon? Shall we introduce her to your dad? Then you could have her for a stepmum!'

All his mates laughed. I saw that Holly was smirking again too.

I gritted my teeth. That's when I started to feel sick. My head started to hurt and I felt a bit dizzy.

I picked up my schoolbag and pushed past them, out of the room. I really didn't feel well. And I started to think of all the terrible illnesses I could have that would mean I'd never be able to come back to school ever again.

'Juliette, I think I might have meningitis,' I said, dumping my schoolbag on the floor and flopping down on to the settee as soon as I got home. 'I've got a terrible headache and I feel really sick. I think maybe I've got a temperature.'

Juliette, who was doing a pile of ironing, put down the iron and came to feel my forehead with the back of her hand. Juliette is twenty-two and really pretty. She's got short blonde hair, cropped just like the models in *Vogue* magazine, and blue eyes with long dark eyelashes. I wish *I* looked more like Juliette. I've got brown eyes and brown hair that's dead straight and comes to my shoulders, and people are always saying that I look really pale.

'You don't feel hot,' Juliette said, removing her hand from my brow.

'That's because I'm cold,' I said, shivering abruptly. 'I'm going to bed. Will you tell Dad I'm not well when he comes in.' I made a big thing of dragging myself off the settee.

'When I've finished this, I will come and see what you want,' Juliette called after me.

I thought the very least she could have done was make sure I didn't faint on the stairs but then Juliette never seems to make a fuss of me that way. No one does. Dad just gets all panicky whenever I'm ill and Matthew just goes, 'Yuck. Germs!' and keeps out of my way. I reckon if my mother was here, she'd make a *huge* fuss of me. My photo of my mother stands right by my bed and when I'm in bed I talk to her and she's always really understanding. I told her about today as I got undressed, and about how sick I felt, and I knew she thought that I should definitely stay off for the rest of the week and get myself truly better.

I got into bed and rested my head against the pillow. I felt thirsty.

'*Darling, I think you should be drinking plenty of fluids,*' my mother said, smiling at me silently.

I climbed out of bed and headed groggily for the landing. 'JULIETTE!' I yelled. 'I want a drink!'

Juliette poked her head out of the living room and glared at me. 'Juliette, will you *please* bring me a drink,' she corrected me, sternly, like being polite really mattered when you were dying of meningitis.

'Orange squash, *please*,' I croaked, swaying dangerously at the top of the stairs.

Juliette sighed, loudly. 'You had better go back to bed. I will bring it up to you.'

I felt tears prick the backs of my eyes. Juliette didn't care about me. I was just a way of making money as far as she was concerned. I ran back to my bedroom and slammed the door. By the time Juliette reached me I was buried under the covers and pretending to be asleep.

'Esmie, here is your drink.' I heard it clink against my mother's picture as she set it down.

I could hear her standing there trying to work out if I really was asleep. I heard her starting to walk out of the room when I felt overcome by a surge of anger. I sat bolt upright in bed. 'Don't bother checking to see if I'm still *alive* or anything, will you?!' I snarled.

She looked shocked. 'Still alive?'

'Yes. I mean, people can die pretty fast from meningitis!'

'Meningitis?' She looked even more puzzled.

'That's right! I mean you're not a doctor, are you? You don't know for sure that I *haven't* got meningitis!'

'Esmie, why are you behaving like this? You

are not so sick to have meningitis. Something has happened to make you like this. What is it?' She came and stood close to my head, so close that she was standing in front of my glass of orange and the photo of my mother. 'Tell me,' she said, crouching down by my bed and touching my head. 'What is wrong?'

I stared at her. I felt all funny inside.

I opened my mouth to say something angry and instead I burst into tears.

Juliette was really different from all our other au pairs right from the beginning. From the day she arrived she chatted to Dad in a way that none of the others ever did. For instance she chatted to him about why she reckoned he never had any success in his relationships. Dad has dated a few women in the past few years but nothing's ever lasted more than a few months. In fact, mostly you're talking weeks, not months. He hadn't gone out with anyone in ages, and then, a few weeks after Juliette arrived, he got set up on a blind date.

The date was arranged by one of Dad's friends. When Dad got home from that evening, it was so early that we were all still up. Dad looked positively traumatized, and Juliette made him relate the whole encounter over a soothing mug of cocoa. I was really pleased. Normally I never get to hear anything about Dad's dates. It sounded like this one had been going all right until the part where his date had asked about my mother and Dad had replied that she was the most beautiful creature he'd ever met and the one great love of his life (or something really slushy like that).

Juliette had gasped in horror. 'But that is *terrible*! It is no wonder you put her off!'

'Well anything else would be a lie!' Dad replied, stubbornly, flushing a little. 'And lying is no way to start off a relationship!'

'Well, you will never start a relationship unless you lie about *this*! Can you not think of something less . . . less *aggressive* . . . to say to these poor women if they are unfortunate enough to ask?'

'You don't mean *aggressive*, Juliette, you mean *passionate*!' I put in, helpfully, but everyone ignored me.

'You could always tell them she was . . . I don't know . . . *sweet*!' volunteered Matthew, who was taking advantage of Dad's temporary state of distraction by standing in front of the fridge with the door open, swigging back orange juice straight from the carton.

'Holly's mum says it's an insult to be called

sweet unless you're lying in a pram wearing a bonnet,' I chipped in again. I turned pointedly to address Juliette. '*She* reckons Dad mucks up all his dates because deep down he's *scared* of falling in love again.'

'Holly's mother should mind her own business,' Dad grunted.

'But there is sense in what she says, no?' Juliette insisted. 'It is scary to fall in love. Especially when you have lost someone.'

Dad visibly swallowed. He never talks about losing my mother. He talks a lot about being *with* her, but never about losing her. Juliette says it's typically English not to want to talk about the feelings that you have deep inside. I'm not sure if it's typically English but I am sure that it's typically *Dad*.

Anyway, Juliette had certainly changed things in our house. She was a lot more interfering than all our other au pairs, and sometimes I worried that Dad wouldn't be able to take it any more and would send her back to France. For one thing, she was always suggesting ways in which Dad could spend more one-to-one time with Matthew in order to promote male bonding.

'Who does she think she is? Mary Poppins?' Dad grumbled, the last time Juliette interfered in one of his disagreements with my brother.

'I can just imagine you flying across from France underneath your umbrella,' I told her now, as she gave me a hug and asked me what the matter was. But I couldn't tell her about what had happened in French today. She might go and tell Dad. So I just said I didn't feel well.

Juliette sighed. 'Perhaps something very nice will happen soon.' She stroked my hair. 'You never know. Your father is an attractive man. He may very well get married again and then you will have a nice new stepmother. Would you like that?'

'Yes, but Dad won't ever get married again,' I said. 'He still loves my mother too much. He doesn't *want* to replace her with anyone else – at least that's what Holly's mother says.'

'What about Holly's mother?' Juliette asked, suddenly. 'She is single too, is she not?'

'No way!' I shrieked, sitting up in bed and forgetting all about my meningitis. 'There is no way Dad and Holly's mother . . . For one thing Dad hates her!'

'*Hates* her?' Juliette looked even more interested. 'Hate is a very *passionate* emotion, no?'

'You mean *aggressive*, Juliette!' I corrected her, but she just smiled, like she knew things that I didn't about life in general.

'I know exactly what I mean,' she said, firmly. 'Now you – with your bad head – should get some rest, I think.' And she winked at me as she left my room.

My Mum's from Planet Pluto

Yet another brilliant story from

Gwyneth Rees

1

'Daniel, I don't see how you can write an essay when you're not even concentrating on it,' Mum said crossly.

It was three weeks after we'd moved house and I was perched on the settee with my feet on the coffee table, trying to watch *Neighbours* and do my summer project. I'd been getting along quite well until Mum came into the room. Mum has this annoying habit of planting herself between me and the television set whenever I'm trying to watch TV and do my homework at the same time. I'm perfectly capable of doing both, but Mum refuses to believe that.

My mum, who's called Isabel, is a teacher and you might think that since she spends all day at work lecturing children she'd want to give it a rest when she comes home, but you'd be wrong. Mum never bats an eyelid if I moan at her for being all teachery at home. She just replies that she likes to get in as much *practice* as possible (especially in the summer holidays, when she might get out of the habit), so isn't it lucky that she's got me?

She said something else which I didn't hear because I was too caught up in listening to *Neighbours*. Some psychotic madman had taken everybody hostage in the coffee shop three episodes ago. He said he'd planted a bomb in there and he was going to set it off if the police didn't meet his demands. Now the police were saying it was just a hoax and they were about to storm the building. The thing was, in the previous episode they'd actually shown this bomb, ticking away under one of the tables, so you knew that it wasn't really a hoax. Any minute now the bomb was going to go off and there were going to be cappuccinos and blown-up bodies flying about all over the place. I leaned sideways in an attempt to see past Mum.

'You didn't hear a word of what I just said, did you?' Mum accused me, shifting her position in order to block the TV more effectively. She had raised her voice so I couldn't hear what the coffee-shop hijacker was saying to the pregnant lady who was screaming because she was about to give birth to twins and he still wouldn't let her out of the shop.

'Shush, Mum . . .' I looked up at her in alarm, realizing my mistake immediately.

'I beg your pardon?' Her brow had furrowed and her eyes were glinty. 'You watch far too much television, Daniel!' She reached behind her and switched it off.

'*Mum!*' I yelled.

'I was *saying*,' she continued doggedly, 'that the *beginning* of any piece of writing has to grab the attention if you want your reader to carry on reading it.'

'Mrs Lyle has *got* to carry on reading it,' I pointed out, staring crossly at the blank TV screen. 'It's her job!'

Mum winced, as if I had just reminded her of a very painful fact. That didn't shut her up though. Sighing a sigh of great sympathy for Mrs Lyle, my new head of year, and all other teachers including herself, she continued, 'And that is precisely why you should try to hand in something that is not *too* unbearable to read. A little effort is what's required, Daniel. A little concentration.' She was looking at me as though she thought I was a lost cause. 'Honestly, I know your father doesn't think you've got that attention deficit disorder or whatever it's called, but I'm really not so sure!'

That made me see red. My concentration – or lack of it – is something Mum's been harping on about forever and even Dad gets cross with her sometimes because he says her expectations are too high. He told her that when he thought I wasn't listening one time. (He'd never say that if he thought I *was* listening because he believes that parents should always present a united front – even if they're both wrong.)

'There's nothing wrong with *my* head . . .' I said sharply.

Mum gave me a surprised – and hurt – look and I instantly felt guilty. We don't normally talk about the times when Mum's been ill. The last time she'd had to be admitted to a psychiatric hospital was seven years ago when my sister, Martha, was born.

I tried to make myself feel better by telling myself I didn't care if I hurt Mum's feelings. After all, she shouldn't say horrible things about me if she doesn't want me to say stuff back.

'All I'm trying to do is encourage you, Daniel,' Mum said, softly now. 'But if you don't care what Mrs Lyle thinks of your work, then that's your look-out.' And she left the room.

'I *don't* care what Mrs Lyle thinks!' I called out after her, because now that she'd reminded me about my new school, I could get angry with her again. After all, it was her fault we'd had to move here.

I looked down at the empty page of my new jotter. I *would* have minded what my class teacher at my *old* school thought because I liked her and I liked my old school. But Mrs Lyle was just a name to me because term hadn't even started back yet and, in any case, I thought it was really dumb of her to send out letters to all the Year Sevens who were going to be starting secondary school for the first time in September, asking them to prepare an introductory essay about themselves over the summer. Even Dad had commented that he thought it was a bit zealous of her, although he'd supported Mum in insisting I do it just the same.

I turned the TV back on and threw my homework jotter on the floor.

Before we'd moved, Mum had been Deputy Head at a secondary school on the other side of the city from where we lived. She had gone for several interviews over the last year and when she finally got offered her very first head teacher's job, I was busy congratulating her like everybody else until I asked whereabouts in the city her new school actually was, and she told me it was on the south coast. The thing was, that was miles away. We'd driven to the south coast one summer for a holiday and it had taken us a whole day to get there.

The really annoying thing was that nobody else in my family seemed to mind as much as me. My dad, who's called Malcolm, said he'd always secretly fancied living by the sea. He's a GP and he joked that there'd be plenty of work for him since seaside towns are full of doddery old people who have to go and see their doctors a lot. My little sister, Martha, liked the idea of living near the beach too. I was the one who hated the idea of leaving our old place the most – and *then* I found out that in our new town I'd be expected to go to the same school as Mum. I begged and begged to be allowed to go to a different school, even if it meant travelling on six different buses every morning to get there. Mum and Dad did give it some thought, but in the end they said that the school where Mum would be working was far and away the best school in the area and that they didn't feel they should make any sacrifices where my education was concerned. Dad was sympathetic but said he was sure that I had what it took to cope and Mum promised that she'd try to be as little of an embarrassment to me as possible (which, when you consider what happened later, turned out to be the biggest joke ever).

I couldn't get back into *Neighbours* properly after that, so when Mum came back into the room, I looked up from the TV immediately.

She didn't say anything about the television being back on. 'Come on. It's about time we took those membership forms back to the library. There might be time for you to choose a book today. We can pick Martha up from her singing class on the way back.'

Martha, my little sister, is seven-and-a-half (she'd want you to remember the half) and she's the sort of little girl that aunties and grannies and other people's mothers all say they want to take home and keep. I've got to admit that she does look really cute. She doesn't look like Mum or Dad or me because we're all dark and she's got fair hair. It's bobbed at her shoulders and she's got these big blue eyes and pink cheeks with dimples. She's always playing some daft pretend game or other and trying to get me to join in. That's unless she's got her new friend Sally with her, in which case she screams at me to go away if I try and set foot in her room. The summer singing class had been Mum's idea. When Martha had protested that she *couldn't* sing, Mum had said that that was an excellent reason then for joining a singing class, wasn't it? I knew the real reason Mum wanted us to join things was so we'd make friends quickly. She'd tried to get me to join some things too, but so far I'd resisted.

As we drove to the library, I stared grumpily out of the car window. I was thinking about how I didn't know a single other person who lived here and how all I wanted was to start at the secondary school in our old town with my old friends. My best friend, Mark, was going there and since our surnames both start with the letter M – mine is MacKenzie and his is Morrison – we thought we might get put in the same classes for stuff, though I wasn't sure if that was how they sorted things out in secondary school. Still, if they did it on academic ability, Mark and I should still have been in the same classes. Except for Maths. Mark's a lot better than me at Maths. And I'm better at creative writing. At least, I am when I'm in the right mood.

'I only wanted to see what happened,' I complained crossly to my mother.

'Sorry?' Mum was concentrating on fiddling with the radio, which was making a horrible crackling noise.

'In *Neighbours*. I only wanted to see who got blown up.'

'Oh, you and your television, Daniel,' Mum said, frowning as a plop of seagull pooh landed on the windscreen. 'It's not good for you. In fact, we should probably get rid of the TV set completely. Maybe that way we'd get you to read some books.'

'NO!' I protested. I know it sounds crazy but the TV seemed to have become really important to me ever since we'd moved. It was very comforting, somehow, to watch the same characters and same stories carrying on as normal when everything in *my* life had completely changed. I sometimes wished I could jump inside the television set and stay there. Or that I could just switch off my real life whenever I got fed up with it, the same way you can switch off a TV programme you don't like.

Mum was looking for a place to park outside the library.

'You can never find anywhere in this street. Get your head out of the way, please, Daniel. I can't see.' She said a rude word as another car beat her to the parking space she'd just spotted. 'Listen, why don't I just let you out of the car here and you can hand in the forms and choose a book while I go and pick up Martha? I'll meet you here again in twenty minutes. OK?'

'Mum—' I wanted to ask her again about the television, to make sure she wasn't really considering getting rid of it.

'And make sure you pick a book that you're actually going to read.'

I knew it was no use pursuing the subject of television when Mum's mind was on books. I got out of the car, slamming the door a lot harder than I needed to.

Sometimes Mum really makes me mad. I know she only wants what she thinks is best for me, but the trouble is that what *she* thinks is best isn't always what *I* think is best. Dad's no help because he agrees with her most of the time – just for a quiet life, I reckon. He even lets her tell him what she thinks is best for *him*, though a lot of the time he just goes and does the opposite when she's not looking.

Well, Mum isn't always right, at least not about me. For one thing, she thinks I hate going to the library, but actually I like it.

The library is probably about the only place in our new town that I think is an improvement on our old one. The library where we used to live was a large, airy, modern building on one level with lots of skylight windows. When it was raining, the rain used to make a terrific clattering noise on those windows. The library here is an old building – Mum says it's at least a hundred years old – that must have once been a very grand private house. I like to imagine it how it used to be, with the big reception area as the main entrance hall, with a maid coming to take your coat and a butler appearing to announce you. There's a wide, twisting, marble staircase that leads up to the reference section, and I could almost see all the ladies sweeping down it in their big, fancy ballgowns, and hear the music as everyone waltzed around the room in the adult reading section or sipped champagne served from silver trays in the children's corner.

That afternoon was the second time I'd been there. The first time we'd popped in quickly to collect the membership forms. There was nobody at the reception desk when I walked in now. Maybe they were busy putting books away or something. I put the completed forms on the desk and went to have a look in the junior readers' section.

I found a book and took it over to the children's corner where there were some little kids' seats. I sat down, opened the book at the first page and started to read. I always try to read at least the first page, and if possible the whole first chapter, of any book to make sure I really like it before I take it out of the library, because last time I got bored with a book halfway through and gave up reading it, Mum seized upon the fact like it was a major piece of evidence in a courtroom trial: 'This just proves what I've been saying all along! You're losing the art of reading! It's all that passive entertainment you get from sitting in front of the television, that's what it is! It's making your brain lazy!' And she wouldn't let me watch any more TV until I'd finished the book and told her the entire plot.

But I don't mind reading if it's a good book. Good books are just as easy to escape into as television – better in our house, because my mum doesn't keep interrupting all the time. I was just starting to get interested in this one when the library door banged shut and loud footsteps sounded on the wooden floor.

A female voice boomed out, sounding slurred. 'Getchyourself a book then, Abby. Hurry up.' I was still getting used to the way people speak here. They have funny voices which Dad says are on account of the flat vowel sounds they have instead of the nicer bouncier ones we use in the north. Though Dad suggested I shouldn't actually point that out to anyone when I started at my new school. As if I'd be that stupid.

'It's OK, Mum. I just need to hand these in.' A girl about my age came into view. She had straight, shoulder-length, light-brown hair and a suntanned face. She was wearing a long brown cotton skirt, a red top and black trainers with red laces. She clutched two books against her chest as she glanced around for the librarian, who still wasn't behind her desk.

The girl's mother pushed past her. She had a puffy red face and short untidy hair. She started to walk clumsily towards the children's section, where I was sitting. 'Look at these liddle plashtic seats – you have to have a liddle bottom to sit on them!' She laughed loudly. Her breath, now that she was close to me, smelt like my Uncle Robert's does when he's had too much beer at Christmas.

I jumped up and my chair fell over. I felt myself flush.

The woman laughed as I bent down to pick it up. The girl called Abby came over to her then and grabbed her arm. Her face was bright red too – with embarrassment at having a mum like that, I reckoned – and she avoided looking at me. 'C'mon, Mum. We have to get back.'

But the woman had already plonked herself down on the rug where some toddlers' books had been left out. 'Look at this!' she said, lifting one up, dangling it by a corner for a moment, then dropping it noisily on to the floor.

The girl saw me staring at her mother and glared at me. 'What are *you* looking at?'

'Nothing,' I said, quickly moving to leave. I hurried over to the bookshelves and put my book back.

Mum was waiting outside for me in the car and Martha was waving to me from the back seat. I waved back. I might moan about my little sister, but she thinks I'm great and that makes her pretty nice to be around most of the time.

Now, as I climbed into the car, I glanced back at the library steps and saw the girl called Abby and her mother come out. I wondered if Abby had a dad. I hoped so, because maybe her dad could help her with her mum.

I looked across at *my* mum, suddenly feeling much less angry with her. Mum always *looks* good no matter what. She's got these dark-blue eyes that Dad says come from her Irish ancestors and lots of thick dark hair which she only ties back when she's at work. People sometimes turn to have a second look at her in the street, though she doesn't seem to notice that. All Mum notices about herself is that she's plumper than she wants to be, which she's always blaming on the lithium. That's the name of the medication she has to take every day to stop getting ill again like she was before. The lithium keeps the chemicals in her brain from getting unbalanced. We've all got chemicals in our brain but some people's work better than other people's. That's how Mum explained it to me one time. You'd think Dad would explain it since he's the doctor in our family, not her, but Dad never likes me asking questions about Mum's illness. Anyway, the lithium tablets Mum takes keep her brain chemicals working the same as everybody else's, but one of the side effects of the medication is that it makes her put on weight more easily. Mum hates that. I've told her lots of times that she's not *horrendously* fat, but she just says, 'Gee, thanks, Daniel,' and carries on glaring at herself in the mirror.

'Mum, I'm sorry about before,' I said now, as I fastened my seatbelt.

'I'm sorry too,' Mum said. 'Now . . . is this

coming-out-of-the-library-with-no-book an act of rebellion, or could you just not find a good one?'

I grinned and said that there just hadn't been any good ones and she said, 'What? In the whole library?' But I could tell she wasn't really angry with me.

Then we both listened while Martha told us how one of the boys had made a bad smell in her singing class and everyone had had to hold their noses while they were singing.

By the time we got home, I was feeling much more chilled about everything and I cheered up even more when I saw that Dad's car was back in the driveway. He had been to visit a couple of GP practices that afternoon to see about applying for a new job.

The chilled feeling didn't last though. It was while Martha and I were in the kitchen raiding the cupboard for crisps that Mum and Dad asked us to sit down because they had something important to tell us.

'Good or bad?' I asked, swinging my kitchen chair back on two legs and banging it down again.

'Just sit still and *listen* for a minute, will you, Daniel . . .' Dad said, sounding impatient, which made me stop fidgeting straight away, because Dad hardly ever sounds like that.

And that's when he told us that he was going to New Zealand for two months – and that he was leaving a week on Saturday.

2

'Daniel, you've been on that phone long enough!'

It was the following morning and Dad was running a bath for Martha. Mum had gone up to the hospital for an outpatient appointment. This was her first appointment since we'd moved and the reason it had come so promptly was because Dad had phoned up and spoken to the psychiatrist himself.

I ignored Dad and carried on talking to my friend Mark from back home. If I was still living at our old place, I'd be down at the park playing football with him right now. We played football nearly every day last summer holidays. I was telling Mark what Dad had told us yesterday – that he had decided to postpone starting a new job here in order to go to New Zealand to visit his mother one last time. Our grandmother, who I'd only ever met three times because she emigrated with my aunt the year before I was born, was diagnosed with cancer last year. We'd already been on this big family holiday to New Zealand last summer to see her, and she'd looked perfectly OK to me. I hadn't expected her to look OK. I thought it was scary because it meant that lots of other people who looked OK could really have a cancer growing inside them. I kept asking Dad how I could tell if *I* had one and in the end he got really upset and shouted at me.

Mum had come to talk to me afterwards. (Usually it's the other way round – Mum shouts at me and Dad's the one who comes to talk to me later.) Mum said he'd shouted because he was only just managing to bear the fact that his mother was dying and that right now he didn't have any strength left to imagine me – his child – as anything but immortal.

That set me off thinking, I remember. I thought about how when Dad and I had watched the DVD of *Highlander* together – where the guy is immortal and can't ever die – Dad had said that being immortal would be the worst thing ever. He'd said he couldn't imagine anything more awful than having to watch everyone you loved grow old and die while never getting to rest in peace yourself. So I seriously doubted that Dad would really want me to be immortal.

But before I could say any of this, Mum had added, 'Daniel, your father is hurting really badly inside right now. So don't just blurt things out like you usually do. *Think* first. Please.'

So I did think and I did my best to be really nice

to Dad the whole of the rest of the time we were in New Zealand. I made him drinks with all different types of fruit juice in them and called them funny names like Bloody Malcolm (that was orange juice mixed with tomato juice) and Bogeyman Surprise (that was a green one with kiwis and bananas in it). And I made a special effort to be extra polite to my gran, even though I've always found her a bit strict and scary. I even pretended not to mind the fact that she said Martha could have her china doll when she died, whereas I wasn't getting anything.

Anyway, the doctors didn't think my gran would last this long, but since she had – and it was going to be her seventy-fifth birthday at the end of September – Dad had decided he wanted to go and see her again. He'd talked it over with Mum, who was really supportive of him going. Mum's an only child and so were both her parents, so she didn't have any family left after they died when she was in her twenties and she's always saying how she wishes she'd spent more time with them.

Dad had booked his flight for the Saturday after we started at our new schools.

'It's a bummer you can't go with him,' Mark said when I told him all this on the phone.

'I know,' I agreed.

'I've got to go now,' Mark added. 'I promised I'd be at Billy's house by half-ten . . .' He sounded a bit awkward again, like he had at the beginning of our conversation. It had been fine once we'd got going, but somehow it had seemed to take us both a little while to start chatting as easily to each other as we always used to. I don't know why. Mark had even said, 'How are you?' when he first came to the phone, really politely, like I was a complete stranger. I mean, we absolutely never asked each other how we were – not unless one of us was off sick with chickenpox or something. And now he was in a rush to meet Billy, who Mark had always said got on his nerves before when he tried to hang out with the two of us.

'DANIEL!' Dad shouted down the stairs.

'See you, Mark,' I said, slamming down the phone and instantly blaming my dad for our conversation having to end before I was ready. Feeling angry with Mark wasn't an option. I missed him too much.

'I thought it was just teenage girls who spent ages on the telephone,' Dad said lightly. 'And I thought I asked you to wash up the breakfast things *before* you phoned Mark.'

'*Mum* stays on the phone much longer than that!' I snapped.

Dad looked surprised. '*Mum* is one of the people in this house who pays the phone bill. *She* can stay on the phone however long she likes.'

'Fine. *I'll* start paying the phone bill too then. You can take it out of my pocket money – there's nothing else to spend it on here anyway!'

'Daniel . . . stop being silly . . .' Dad came down

the stairs towards me. Unlike Mum, he hardly ever loses his temper with me no matter how obnoxious I'm being. He stooped to pick up my trainer, which had been lying on the stairs for the past two days, and handed it to me. 'Come on . . . It'll be easier once school starts back. You'll make some new friends.'

'No I won't,' I snarled. 'Not when everyone finds out my mum is the new head! Anyway, *you* don't like it here either!'

'Huh?' He put his hand out to stop me as I made to push past him up the stairs. 'What do you mean?'

'I heard you on the phone the other night to Uncle Robert. You told him you missed your old job much more than you thought you would and on a rainy day this has to be the dreariest little town you've ever encountered in all your forty-three years!' Uncle Robert is Dad's best friend and he's the nearest thing to a proper uncle we've got. Dad had been on the phone to him the other night for even longer than I'd just been on the phone to Mark.

Dad let go of my arm, looking uncomfortable. He pulled a face, then gave me a weak grin. 'Didn't I say *dearest*, not *dreariest*?'

'No you did not!' I snarled, pushing past him to get upstairs, where I collided with Martha on the landing as she came stumbling out of her bedroom in her pink pyjamas to see what all the noise was about.

'DAD-DY!' She let out a deafening shriek as if I'd just tried to murder her or something.

I glared at her. After all, I hadn't bumped into her on purpose, had I? Then I saw that she was looking past me, into the bathroom. Foamy water was gushing down the side of the bath on to the carpet.

As Dad came thudding up the stairs, I decided this would be a good time to escape. I grabbed my favourite jacket from the floor of my bedroom and paused for a moment to look at myself in the wardrobe mirror as I put it on. I used to have a much chubbier face when I was younger, but I reckon I look much better now that you can see my cheekbones. I've got dark-brown cropped hair that I never think needs combing (though Mum always makes me anyway) and blue eyes like Mum's. I reckoned I looked cool enough to go out and about on my own in my new neighbourhood. Normally I'd have asked Dad before I took off anywhere but right then I felt like it was my decision, not his.

In the bathroom, Dad and Martha had turned off the taps and were attempting to mop up the flood with a whole heap of towels. They didn't notice me as I trod lightly across the landing and down the stairs.

At the very bottom, I yelled up at them as loudly as I could, 'I'M GOING OUT! SEE YOU LATER!'

Before Dad had a chance to reply I slammed the door and was gone. And I didn't feel the least bit guilty about leaving the breakfast things for him to do. After all, he wouldn't have to do *any* washing-up for a whole two months when he went off without us to New Zealand, would he?

A selected list of titles available from
Macmillan Children's Books

The prices shown below are correct at the time of going to press.
However, Macmillan Publishers reserves the right to show new retail
prices on covers, which may differ from those previously advertised.

Gwyneth Rees

The Mum Hunt	978-0-330-41012-0	£5.99
The Mum Detective	978-0-330-43453-9	£5.99
The Mum Mystery	978-0-330-44212-1	£4.99
My Mum's from Planet Pluto	978-0-330-43728-8	£4.99
The Making of May	978-0-330-43732-5	£5.99

For younger readers

Fairy Dust	978-0-330-41554-5	£4.99
Fairy Treasure	978-0-330-43730-1	£4.99
Fairy Dreams	978-0-330-43476-8	£4.99
Fairy Gold	978-0-330-43938-0	£4.99
Fairy Rescue	978-0-330-43971-8	£4.99
Fairy Secrets	978-0-330-44215-2	£4.99
Mermaid Magic (3 books in 1)	978-0-330-42632-9	£4.99
Cosmo and the Magic Sneeze	978-0-330-43729-5	£4.99
Cosmo and the Great Witch Escape	978-0-330-43733-2	£4.99
Cosmo and the Secret Spell	978-0-330-44216-9	£4.99
The Magical Book of Fairy Fun	978-0-330-44421-7	£4.99
Cosmo's Book of Spooky Fun	978-0-330-45123-9	£4.99

All Pan Macmillan titles can be ordered from our website,
www.panmacmillan.com, or from your local bookshop and
are also available by post from:

Bookpost, PO Box 29, Douglas, Isle of Man IM99 1BQ

Credit cards accepted. For details:
Telephone: 01624 677237
Fax: 01624 670923
Email: bookshop@enterprise.net
www.bookpost.co.uk

Free postage and packing in the United Kingdom